Sullivan Production, LLC

1

Addicted To Love

By

De'Mettrea

Prologue

A'more

I couldn't believe what my life had become. I had gone from being a rich kid from the suburbs to a damn cocaine addict. I had lost the love of my life as well as my son. My father wanted nothing to do with me and my mother tried to help whenever my father wasn't home.

I hadn't seen Trent or my son in almost a year. The words he said to me the last time I talked him would forever be etched in my brain.

"I never want to see you again. You are a poor excuse for a woman and my son will not be raised by you. Stay away from me you selfish bitch!"

You would have thought his words would make me want to get clean, but that was four months earlier and I was still using. All it did was make me sink into a deeper depression. I needed help and I didn't know who to turn too. As I lay on the floor of the drug house, flashbacks of me giving birth to my son, my graduation, Trent's proposal, along with other things ran through my mind. I needed a fix and couldn't get one. I had run through all the money in my account, sold my car for drugs, and I had nothing left.

My body began to shake; I was cold even though it was damn near ninety degrees outside. I sat there going through withdrawals. I wanted it to stop. I wanted to hold my son and lay in Trent's arms. *Lord help me,* I prayed, and then I passed out.

Trent

When I got the call from Eddie telling me that he had found A'more passed out on the floor, I got emotional. It was embarrassing as hell but at the same time, I knew I needed to get to her and help her. As much as I wanted to leave her ass there, I couldn't. We had a bond that wouldn't allow me to turn my back on her. I still loved her and was going to do everything I could to help her.

I dropped my son off at his godmother Chante's house and made my way to where A'more was.

When I pulled up Eddie was waiting outside.

"What's up bruh?" he greeted me.

"What's good man? Where is she?" I asked getting straight to the point.

"She's inside. Look man I know you still love that girl, help her through this shit man. This isn't the A'more we all know. I don't like seeing her like this man."

"Thanks for calling me." I made my way into the house and when I saw A'more lying there, I almost cried. That was my heart right there and I vowed at that moment that I would do everything in my power to help her. I picked her up and took her to my truck. I was taking her to someone that I knew could help her.

"I got you ma, believe that."

I took A'more to my mom's house in Chesterfield. My mom was a nurse and knew exactly what to do to help her detox. By the time I pulled up to my mom's house, A'more was in the back seat throwing up. I got out and helped her out of the car.

"Come on ma, let's get you better." I picked her up and carried her inside.

"Hey Ma." I spoke to my mom who was expecting us.

"Hey sweetie. Take her to the guest room and I'll be right up." I did as she said and took her upstairs and put her in the bed. As I was undressing her, I noticed that she had a fever. That scared the shit out of me. First the vomiting and now she had a fever. I ran downstairs to my mom.

"Ma she has a fever and she was throwing up in the car," I said concerned.

"That's normal with withdrawals, which leads me to believe that she's been going through this for a few days.

"Ok so what do we do now?" I asked.

"You leave and let me do what I do. I'll keep you updated, but you need to be there for Christian." Hearing my son's name let me know I was doing the right thing by helping his mother. I prayed that we would prevail in the end. We had to.

Chapter One

How They Met

Trent

"Damn! Who is lil mama right there?" I asked my boy Raheem. We were chilling, sitting on the hood of his '81 black Cutlass. It was summer time in the D and everyone was out on the block. We were looking at a group of three females walking down the street and one in particular caught my eye. She was a bad bitch. One thing about me, when I saw something I wanted I went after it, and I wanted her.

"That's A'more and her girls, but don't even think about hollering. She be fucking with that nigga Marvin," Raheem responded.

"Fuck that nigga. Hell he owes me money anyway and his chick can be his down payment."

We laughed but I was serious as hell.

"You ain't shit nigga. But anyways, how is that deal going with the barbershops?" Raheem asked me. We had been investing in a few businesses and were doing pretty well profit wise.

"So far so good. If everything goes well tomorrow we should be closing on the location downtown by the end of the week," I responded while still checking out

A'more. She was fine as hell, standing at least 5'7. She had caramel colored skin and long curly hair. She had to be mixed with something, but what I didn't know. I wanted her and vowed to have her sooner rather than later.

"Nigga are you listening to me or are you that damn infatuated with A'more?" Raheem joked.

"Nah, I'm here. Shorty bad as hell though," I responded still looking her way.

"So what's on the floor for tonight?" Raheem asked.

"Shit it don't matter to me. But I'm about to head out. I gotta stop by ma dukes place for a minute. Just hit me up and let me know something."

I gave Raheem a fist pound before hopping in my car. As I pulled off my eyes connected with A'more's and she smiled. I gave her a head nod and thought to myself, *Yeah she's definitely about to be mine.*

*****

A'more

"A'more are you going to Rouge with us? You know Raheem and his crew gonna be there and I'm trying to get with that fine nigga," Chante, one of my best friends asked.

That girl was a mess but she'd had a crush on Raheem for the longest time. From what Lashay told me, she had liked him since she was twelve and he was fifteen, but he had a girl.

"I'm down. I was supposed to hang with Marvin but his ass been acting hella shady lately, so fuck him," I responded as my eyes connected with Trent's. I had never really paid attention to him until then and boy was he fine as hell. I had heard about him and from what I understood, he was a hood legend. Every chick around the way wanted to be on his arm.

We were chilling on Chante's porch watching the neighborhood come alive. There was always some kind of activity going on in the hood. It was good entertainment, especially for me, considering I wasn't from around those parts. Chante was from the hood and I was from the suburbs. We were total opposites but the best of friends. While I was privileged, Chante's mom worked hard every day to provide for her. I was the only child and my father gave me pretty much whatever I wanted.

At seventeen, I stood 5'7, 135 pounds, and was what most called a bad bitch. My smooth caramel complexion came from my Italian father and Black mother. Even though I lived in the suburbs, I had a thing for thugs. I liked them rough but also needed them to know when to turn it off and just be a gentleman.

I had been dating Marvin for the past six months and at first, it was everything I wanted, but I was getting bored. I wasn't feeling the situation with Marvin and was ready to end things. I knew he had been cheating and I was sick of his shit. Now don't get it twisted, I was far from naïve. I knew a man was going to be a man but keep that shit tight. I shouldn't have had to find out about his extracurricular activities from others. At least be clean about that shit and keep it under wraps.

"Girl everybody is going to be there tonight. They're having the race tonight. So you know we have to be front and center," Lashay responded. The race was a bunch of hood niggas showing off their cars, old school and new. They wanted to show that they had the best ride and baddest chick riding shotgun.

"Fa'sho!" Chante replied a little too hyped.

Lashay and I attended the same high school in Bloomfield Hills, but Lashay lived in the hood as well. Her parents wanted her to attend a good school so she was bused all the way out to go to school. That was how we met and we'd been hanging tight since ninth grade, along with Chante.

"Well we should be ready to leave around six," Chante said.

"That's cool with me. I'm gonna head home and change and I'll be back to pick y'all up," I told the girls as I headed to my 2013 Mercedes GLK, courtesy of my parents.

When I pulled up to the house both my parent's cars were there. I hoped that they didn't give me a problem with going out that night. My mom was cool but my dad was overprotective. When he did have the time, he kept me from doing a lot of things.

"Hey Mom," I spoke as I went in the house.

"Hey sweetie. How was your day?" my mom asked.

"It was cool. I'm actually headed out with the girls tonight if that's ok with you," I replied.

"That's fine honey."

My mom didn't really care what I did as long as I didn't get in trouble doing it. Nina Mancini was a laid-back woman and pretty much had nothing to say about anything. It was only when my father said something did my mom have a problem. I loved my mom but she had no backbone when it came to my dad. I always told myself that I wouldn't be a weak woman. I would always have a voice when it came to a man.

Dad was probably in his office working as usual. Armando Mancini was a Kingpin and stayed too busy to notice anything I did. He was normally too busy worrying about his money, but when he did notice me, boy did he go overboard.

I headed upstairs to find something to wear. I wanted to look cute but not slutty. I believed a woman could look sexy without revealing too much. After looking through my closet for a good twenty minutes, I finally found an outfit. I decided on a pair of black Levi's and a red baby tee with the black and red Jordan 11's. I pulled my long hair up into a messy bun and applied some M.A.C. lip-gloss.

I called Chante and Lashay on three-way to see if they were ready to go.

"Hey chicas, y'all ready to roll?" I asked when they answered the phone.

"Yup," Chante replied.

"Sure am," Lashay said.

"Okay I'm on my way." I hung up, grabbed my purse and keys, and headed out the door.

****

"Damn it's live as hell up here. All these fine men, lawd help me," Lashay fanned herself. She was known to be dramatic.

"There are a few cuties up in here," I replied looking around. Truth was I was looking for Trent.

"Girl please. You know Marvin will get all up in that ass if he catches you looking at another man," Chante replied.

"Whatever, Marvin's ass ain't gon' do a damn thing. Shit, his ass hasn't been around enough lately anyways to even notice me looking at anyone. Word is he been with his baby mama all week. So he can stay with her for all I care."

I knew about Marvin's baby mama and that wasn't an issue because I loved him, but lately he had been neglecting me and just disrespectful, so I was ready to move on without him. Hell, I was too young for all the drama. I was about to graduate and head off to Spellman in Atlanta.

"Damn really? He slipping big time," Lashay said with a concerned look on her face.

"It's all good."

I tried to act as if it didn't bother me but my girls knew better. Even though Marvin was acting an ass, I loved him. Or at least I thought I did.

"Girl forget Marvin. Trent sexy ass is checking you out." Chante was too excited as if she was the one he was checking out. I think she really just wanted to get close to Raheem.

"Girl bye, that boy ain't thinking about me," I said while looking up at Trent.

"He is too, and if you know like I know, you better get up on that. He's a boss ass nigga and very much wanted around the way. Ya better snatch his fine ass up girl," Lashay replied.

I looked in his direction again and he indeed was looking at me. He smiled and I returned the gesture.

He motioned for me to come to him and of course, the girls got geeked for me.

"Oh God, he wants me to go over there," I said, covering my mouth with my hand.

"What the hell are you waiting for? Get yo ass over there," Chante scolded like she was my mother. She pushed me in his direction. Could she have been any more obvious?

I slowly walked over to where Trent was chilling with his boys.

"What's good lil' mama?" Trent asked when I got within arm's reach of him.

I couldn't get over how fine he was. He had to be about 6 feet even and had smooth chocolate skin. He had long hair that was braided to the back, a goatee, and a full beard, which was a big turn on for me. I loved a man with facial hair.

"Nothing much, just hanging with my girls," I responded while pointing back at my girls.

"That's what's up. So where ya man at ma?" He was looking dead in my eyes and making me nervous as hell.

"That's a good question that I wish I had the answer to," I replied, trying to focus my attention on something other than his luscious ass lips.

"Damn ma, it sounds like that nigga fucking up. I guess that means there's room for me to step in," he said as he stepped in my personal space. I could smell the mint from the gum he was chewing, that's how close he was. I wanted to suck his tongue just to taste the flavor. Damn I was tripping hard over dude and I didn't even know him.

"Uh uh playa, that's not what that means."

I smiled as I looked up in his face. I playfully pushed him back. He towered over my little frame.

He stepped forward, bent down, and whispered in my ear. "Tell that fuck boy it's over because you belong to me now." He grabbed me by my belt loops and pulled me closer to him.

Damn the smell of his cologne had me gone. Marvin was officially pushed to the back of my mind. There was something about Trent's take-charge attitude that had me intrigued. I didn't know how it was going to play out, but fuck it; I was throwing caution to the wind. Somehow, I knew I was playing with fire messing with him, but I wanted to be burned.

"What makes you think I wanna be yours?" I asked while I was still in his arms.

"The fact that I'm holding on to you and you ain't moved nor asked me to let you go. Stop fronting ma, cause you want me just as much as I want you."

That nigga read the hell out of me. He was right though. Trent was sexy as hell. He was tall and buff, just like I liked 'em. And my God, the boy was tatted up. That shit was too damn sexy. He had a whole sleeve and that was just what I could see with his shirt on. That nigga had me damn near drooling.

"Yeah ok, you feeling yourself a little too much. But you got that," I replied still playing hard to get.

Before I knew it, he bent down and kissed me. To my surprise, I didn't pull away but I welcomed it and I felt like I had died and gone to heaven. For a good two minutes, we stood there tonging each other down. We didn't give a damn that we were in a parking lot full of people.

"Damn ma. You about to have a nigga sprung already," he said and we laughed.

"Aye A'more, what's up with ya girl Lashay?" Brandon asked me.

"Why don't you go see," I replied.

"Fa'sho!" he responded as he walked away.

"Where ya phone at?" Trent asked me. I passed him my iPhone and he programmed his number in it before calling his phone.

"Here." He passed it back to me. "Well I gotta handle some business but I wanna get up with you tomorrow, ok?"

"Ok cool," I responded. I hugged him and headed back over to where my girls were standing.

"Get it bitch!" Chante's ass was all kinds of crazy but I loved her.

*****

A month later...

Marvin

I couldn't believe my girl was running around with Trent's ass. Yeah I had been chilling with my baby mama and all, but she still was acting like she didn't have a man. Well I was about to set her ass straight. That was the thing with those young chicks, they needed to be trained how to act.

I pulled up to Chante's house, which was where A'more was known to hang. What do you know; she was chilling on the porch with her hood rat ass friends. I got out of my ride and walked up to her.

"What's up A'more?" I asked.

She looked up at me and rolled her eyes.

Smack!

"Bitch you better show me some damn respect!" I spat. I didn't want to put my hands on her but she had made me go there. I was her man and she was supposed to respect me, not make me look like an ass in front of her girls. I had told her about hanging with them bitches anyway

"What the fuck! Nigga you done lost yo damn mind." Lashay and Chante both jumped up in my face but the look I gave them told them to back the hell up.

"So you running around with other niggas huh? You forgot you had a man?" I yelled.

"Fuck you nigga! You running around with ya bum ass baby mama and all these other hoes."

I was losing my patience with her ass.

"Get the fuck up and let's go now!" She just sat there. I reached down and yanked her ass up.

Click!

"Get ya fucking hands off my girl."

What do you know, that bitch ass nigga Trent was playing Captain Save a Hoe.

"Alright dawg, you got this one." I let her go and turned around to be met with the barrel of a gun.

"I'll be back A'more." I smiled as I walked away.

"Naw homey, don't shit over here belong to you. If I catch you so much as breathing in her space, I'm peeling ya cap back. That's me right there," he pointed at A'more. He had one up on me since my piece was in the car but please believe payback was a bitch.

I got in my ride and headed out with revenge on my mind. I was going to make Trent pay for what he did if it was the last thing I did.

A'more

I couldn't believe that nigga put his hands on me. I was in Chante's bathroom trying to put concealer on my damn face so my parents wouldn't see that shit. I was thankful that Trent was hanging on the block that day. Marvin tried to front on me in front of everybody and got what he deserved.

Knock! Knock!

"Just a minute."

I was trying to finish putting the concealer on when the door opened. Trent walked in and closed the door.

"Come here ma," he said while pulling me into his arms. "I almost killed that nigga for putting his hands on you."

"Yeah he lost his damn mind." I looked Trent in the eyes.

"Why didn't you tell that nigga is was over? You had him thinking y'all was still a couple."

"Not exactly. I haven't seen or talked to him in a few weeks."

"Well he's got the picture now. Come on; let's go to the crib. I wanna chill with you for a while."

We headed out of the bathroom and when we got outside all eyes were on us.

"What the hell y'all looking at?" Trent asked and everybody laughed.

"I'm out y'all. I'll call you later Chante."

"See ya. Don't do anything I wouldn't do," Lashay said as she laughed.

I just smiled at the thought of Trent taking my virginity. I wasn't ready but lord knew when I was, I wanted him to be the one.

*****

Chante

I was happy for my girl. Trent was a good guy and I knew he'd take good care of her. Now if only I could get my hands on Raheem we'd be good. I knew he had a girl but hell; I was around before that chick. It was cool because I vowed one day to have Raheem's sexy ass.

"What you over there thinking about?" Lashay asked bringing me out of my thoughts.

"Raheem's sexy ass."

She shook her head at me. "Girl bye. That man is taken. You need to look elsewhere," she responded.

I knew she was right but there was something about him that I couldn't shake. I had been in love with him since I was eleven and the shit wouldn't go away.

"I hear you girl but damn!"

She laughed. "Anyway, you know Trent giving Big Boy a party this weekend and we are in the building. We need to go grab something to wear."

Trent and his crew always did it big. Big Boy was Brandon's older brother and Brandon was one of Trent's best friends. Big Boy had done a ten-year bid and was touching down Friday.

"You know I'm down." I loved a good party and Trent was known to throw one.

"It's a bet then. We go shopping tomorrow and hopefully we can get A'more's ass from up under Trent to go with us."

"Leave my girl alone. I like Trent for her."

Lashay was my girl but she had a way of throwing shade sometimes. Some of the shit she said didn't sit too well with me. I was gonna have to keep an eye on her ass. I wasn't for that shady shit.

*****

Trent

It was Saturday, the day of my homey Big Boy's party. He had just touched down the day before and I

wanted to make sure shit was nice for him. Big Boy
was an OG. Back in the day, he was the man and we
looked up to him, but he ended up getting caught up
on a weapons charge and being that he had priors,
they gave him fifteen years. Luckily, he only did ten.

I was chilling with my shorty until later. Things
between us were going good. I loved the hell out of
that girl. She was smart and she wasn't a gold digger.
Even though her dad had money, she wasn't stuck up
and I loved that about her.

"So have you decided what you want to do for your
birthday ma?"

Her graduation and birthday were fast approaching. I
wanted to do something special for her because she
deserved it. There were times that I came home to
food waiting in the microwave, my crib cleaned, and
laundry done. The thing about that was she didn't
even live there. I could just imagine what it would be
like for her to live with me.

"Naw. It really doesn't matter. We can go to dinner or
something."

I pulled her up on my chest. "Naw ma, we doing
something nice for ya birthday. Dinner won't cut it."

She smiled and then kissed my lips. "Babe you know
I don't like all that extra stuff," she responded.

"I know. Oh yeah I got you something."

She smiled again and my dick jumped. Damn I wanted her in the worst way but I loved her little ass so much that I was willing to wait until she was ready.

"Where is it?" she got excited.

"Upstairs."

She hopped up off me and ran upstairs as I followed. I took my time getting up there on purpose. I knew she was up there looking for her gift.

While she was in the bedroom looking for her gift, I had grabbed it from the guest room. I was standing in the doorway watching her look. She finally looked up and laughed.

"You play too much." She reached for the gift.

I pulled it out of her reach. "Give me a kiss first," I said with my lips puckered up.

She kissed me and I grabbed her ass with my free hand. We kissed for a good minute before she pulled away and I passed her the gift-wrapped box from Tiffany's.

The look on her face when she opened it was priceless. It was a 2.5-caret princess cut diamond ring.

"Oh God babe! Is this an engagement ring?" she asked still shocked.

"Naw, it's sort of a promise ring. It's my promise to you. I promise always to be there for you as long as you keep it real with me. I love you lil' mama."

She kissed me. "Thanks so much babe. I love it."

"I'm glad. There's much more where that came from if you stick with ya boy." I turned around so that she could get on my back and I carried her back downstairs.

"I'ma stick with you forever boy."

That was music to my ears. I knew without a doubt that was going to be my wife.

*****

"Did you tell ya parents that you were staying the night with Chante?" I asked A'more as we got dressed for the party.

"Yeah. My dad wasn't home but my mom was cool with it. I'm all yours for the night."

I loved the sound of that. But could I handle her being in my bed and not making love to her? That shit was going to be hard as hell. I foresaw a cold shower in my future.

"Come on bae, let's go with yo slow ass," I smacked her on her fat ass and watched it jiggle.

"You play too damn much." She grabbed her purse and we headed out.

It was an all-white event so my baby and me was stunting on those niggas. She wore an all-white Gucci pants suit. The top was backless and she was rocking the hell out of it. Her hair was shaved on one side and she rocked a Mohawk. She sort of reminded me of the singer Cassie, but finer. Yeah I had a bad bitch on my arm.

I kept it simple in a white linen suit, white gators, and a little bling. Not too much, but enough. We hopped in my Maserati and she drove. I just wanted to sit back and let my bae do her thing. She loved that damn car, plus when we pulled up, I wanted everyone to see who was running shit. My baby.

When we pulled up to Club Skyy it was mad crowded. Everybody had come out to welcome Big Boy home. He was a legend so it was only right.

"Come on ma lets go have fun." I escorted A'more in and we headed for the VIP section that was set up for Big Boy.

"What's up y'all? I see my man Trent and his lovely lady walking thru the door so you know what time it is," the DJ announced as we walked thru the door. I got mad love all around the D because I was a real nigga.

It took us a minute because everybody and their mama wanted to say what's up.

After a good five minutes, we finally made our way to the VIP.

"What's good fellas, ladies," I spoke to everyone and introduced A'more to those she didn't know.

"So you're the one that got my little homie so damn chill. You must be a special one to get this nigga to calm down," Big Boy joked.

"She is. This is my heart right here, my ride or die. Aye waiter, let me get a bottle of Ace over here."

We sat and kicked it and everyone was having a good time but there was always somebody in the mix trying to fuck shit up.

"Damn Trent so you cuffing kids now?" I knew that voice without even turning around. Mya.

"Man get the fuck on with that shit yo." I was heated. I was hoping she didn't say anymore shit in front of A'more. Yeah I was still hitting that, but I loved A'more. I mean A'more was still a virgin and a nigga had needs.

"Yeah ok Trent. You think you can just play with people's emotions but ya girl will soon learn wont she?"

I gave that bitch an evil glare that told her she was overstepping her boundaries. The whole time A'more handled it well. Never once did she say anything. She could have gotten hood on Mya's but she didn't.

"Look, get the fuck on somewhere," I told her but she stood there looking at A'more for a minute before walking away. Just when I thought things were good, A'more stood up and walked away.

"Where you going?" I grabbed her arm but she snatched away and gave me a look that said get the fuck on. So I let her go, but kept my eye on her.

She headed towards the door and I knew I had to go after her.

"I'm out y'all. I need to go see where the hell this girl went."

When I got outside, I saw her pulling off. Damn, I was going to have to deal with attitude when I got home. I was fucking Mya's ass up for real. I headed back inside to enjoy the rest of the night. Fuck it. If those bitches wanted to act silly, they could do it by themselves.

A'more.

That nigga had me all the way fucked up. I knew who Mya was but she had stepped out of her lane and the next time I was fucking that bitch up. Only reason she got a pass was because I wasn't a rat bitch that fought in clubs. Please believe her time was coming. That nigga should have kept her in check. Don't step in my lane unless you trying to get run the fuck over, real talk. I was young but I would fuck a bitch up quick.

I was in Trent's bed asleep when he finally walked in the house. I was a light sleeper so I heard him come in. I looked at the clock and it read 4:45. That nigga was trying me. When he walked in the room, I went in on his ass.

"Check this out homeboy. I'm not one for the bullshit. I don't know what you got going on with that bitch but you need to dead it and fast. I will mangle you and that bitch, real talk. She was straight disrespectful and then yo ass come in at 4:45 in the damn morning. Ain't shit open but legs, and being that mine are closed that poses a problem. Ya dig?"

He looked at me like I had two heads but I didn't give a fuck. He wasn't about to play games with me.

"First off, watch ya damn mouth. Second, I don't live with you so I don't have to check in with you. Now far as ol' girl, I handled that shit. Ain't shit popping between me and her."

He took off his clothes, got in bed, and pulled me close. I didn't have shit else to say. He had shut my ass up quick but please believe that I was watching his ass. That definitely didn't go how I planned. That nigga had a take-charge attitude and that turned me the hell on. I knew once we finally did go there that shit was going to be epic.

Raheem

I had a good time at the club. Well besides Michelle's sour ass attitude, and then Chante came looking fine as hell. I didn't know what it is about that girl but I wanted her in the worst way. One problem with that was I had a girl but shit between me and Michelle wasn't kosher. We argued everyday about dumb shit and we didn't even have sex anymore. I didn't know how much longer I was going to deal with that shit.

I had known Chante since we were younger. She was always a cool ass person but I couldn't go there with her because she was too young. But she was about to turn eighteen and that was legal for me to fuck with her. I had just dropped Michelle off and I needed to clear my head, so I called Brandon and told him I was coming through. I knew Trent and A'more were laid up so I wasn't going there. I headed to my boy house to get a good night sleep. There was always one good thing that came out of those; the dreams I had about Chante.

Chapter Two

Love on Top

A'more

It was almost time for my prom and I wanted to go with Trent but that all depended on my daddy. I planned on bringing him to meet Daddy that night and if all went well then we could go shop for my dress.

Trent wasn't as nervous as I was about meeting my daddy. That's because he didn't know my daddy like I did.

"What's wrong baby?" Trent asked me as he ate his food. We were sitting in Denny's having lunch and I sat there picking over my food. I didn't have much of an appetite because I was so nervous.

"I'm just nervous about you meeting Daddy that's all."

He wiped his mouth and looked up at me with that sexy ass smirk that made my panties wet. "Calm down ma. It will be fine. I'm sure pops will like me, cause what's not to like?"

He was so damn cocky and I loved it.

"Well let's get this over with." I stood and pushed my chair in and Trent followed suit. After leaving the tip

and the money for the bill, we left. We headed to my
house ready to face my parents.

*****

I was surprised to see my dad's car parked in the
driveway. I was actually hoping to introduce Trent to
my mom first and then my dad. My mom was the
easy one; it was my dad that was going to give him a
hard time.

"Mom! Dad!" I called out.

"We're in the family room."

"Come on." I dragged Trent into the family room
where my mom was sitting reading a magazine and
my dad was watching the game.

"Mom, Dad, this is Trent."

My dad looked up from the TV. He didn't say
anything for a while. He just looked at Trent like he
was a book he was studying. Then he spoke. "What is
your business with my daughter?" My dad was calm
when he asked the question.

"Well sir, I really care for your daughter and I see
myself with her long term," Trent responded. I could
see the veins in my father's neck pop out.

"No offense son, but my daughter is getting ready to
leave for Atlanta in a few months and I don't need

you or anybody else distracting her from her goals. I really don't think you are the one for her nor do I feel she should be dating. With that being said, you all need to axe this mess ASAP."

My father stood and left out of the room without saying another word. I was speechless.

"Let me go talk to him," I told Trent as I went after my daddy.

I found him downstairs where his gun collection was. That wasn't good. Whenever he went down there, he was ready to kill something.

"Daddy why are you acting like this? You don't even know him," I whined. That usually won my daddy over because I was so spoiled. Unfortunately, that wasn't working that time.

"I don't need to know him. I see right through him. He's a thug and I don't want you seeing him. End of discussion."

"So you don't want me dating someone who's like you is what you're saying?" I challenged.

"That thug is nothing like me." he responded.

"No he isn't. You sell drugs, he doesn't. You're a king pin and he's a business owner. Shall I continue?" I stood up to him unlike my mother.

"Get him out of my house."

"Well I'll be eighteen in two months then what? I'll be able to make my own decisions," I replied.

"As long as I'm taking care of you and paying that high ass tuition at Spellman, then I make your decisions. Now get out!" I couldn't believe my dad was being such an ass. I went back upstairs where Trent was waiting.

"I'm sorry Trent, I'll call you later." He nodded his head understanding. "It's ok ma. He'll come around. I love you and I'll always be here for you." That was why I loved him. He handled things so well, unlike my emotional ass. He left and I was confused on what my next move would be, because my daddy was an important part of my life and so was Trent now. But now it was as if I had to choose and that wasn't fair.

*****

I was getting used to being up under Trent. Although my daddy practically forbade me to see him, I still did. He was much different from Marvin. While Marvin hustled in the streets, Trent turned his hustle into something better. I loved the drive he had. He didn't use that "I'm from the hood so I gotta hustle" line that these niggas used nowadays. If only my daddy got to know him then things would be perfect. My daddy was an important part in my life. For as long as I could remember I had been daddy's little girl. But I was moving into adulthood; I had a good man in my life and my daddy didn't approve.

Addicted To Love   *by Demettrea*

I was lying in bed when Lashay called.

"What's up chick?" I answered.

"Let's go to the mall today, I need some girl time."
Usually when Lashay said she needed girl time she
was having boy problems. So I knew the day was
about to be eventful.

"Cool just give me about an hour and I'll be there."
We hung up and I texted Trent to see what he was
doing today.

Me: Hey love.

Trent: what's yup ma?"

Me: What are you doing today?"

Trent: Working at the barbershop today. You?"

Me: Headed to the mall with the girls. I may stop up
there later.

Trent: Ok. You need some money?

Me: nah, I'm good bae. Love you

Trent: Love you too ma

I got up and got dressed. It was winter in Michigan so
I knew I had to dress for the weather. I wore blue
True religion jeans and a purple sweater that I had
bought the other day from BeBe. I had a ton of shoes
thanks to my shoe fetish, but I decided to wear my
purple Uggs with the bows on the back. I loved those

shoes, that's why I had five pair in different colors. I pulled my hair up into a ponytail and headed out.

When I pulled up to Lashay's house, she was outside arguing with Reggie. I didn't know whether or not to call him her boyfriend or what, because they never defined what they were. They had been messing with each other off and on for about three years.

I just shook my head. Why Lashay continued to go through drama with Reggie is something I will never understand. He was a small time hustler. He was still nickel and diming trying to make it. I got out the car and let my presence be known. I was ready to go and was not up for the bullshit from these two.

"Hey y'all," I spoke. They were still going at it.

"Look Reggie I'm about to go with A'more so bye." She tried to walk away but Reggie snatched her arm.

"I just told ya ass you ain't going no damn where. You always trying to run behind theses bitches instead of chilling with me," he ranted.

"Wait a minute now. Don't disrespect me in my damn face. I haven't done a damn thing to you." That nigga done lost his mind.

"Bitch please. This is between me and my girl so swerve." I looked up at Lashay to see if she was going to say anything. But she never did. What kind of friend would let their nigga be disrespectful to their best friend and not say anything? It was cool though because she just showed me how she got down.

"You know what I'm good on you sweetie. You have fun with ya man." With that being said, I walked away from a four-year friendship. I was so pissed at Lashay it wasn't funny. I decided to head to the barbershop and chill with Trent since my plans fell through.

*****

When I pulled up to the barbershop Trent's Range Rover was parked out front so I knew he was here. He wasn't expecting me till later but I thought I'd surprise him with lunch. I had stopped at New Wave and picked up some catfish for him.

When I walked in all eyes were on me but not for long. Everyone there knew I was Trent's girl.

"Hey Brandon. Is Trent in the office?" I asked.

"Yeah but uh…he should be out in a minute. I'll go and get him," he stuttered.

"Nah that's ok I'll get him." He tried to stop me from going in there. Why, I didn't know but my answer hit me in the face as soon as I turned the knob. Why the hell was Trent's ex Mya in his office and damn near sitting on his lap. He still hadn't noticed me standing in the door. I cleared my throat. I knew something was going on with them but didn't have any proof.

"Hey ma," he said looking at me. Mya turned to look at me and then back at Trent.

"What's this?" I asked.

"Mya was just leaving," Trent said still looking at me.

"Why was she here in the first place? I asked.

"That's none of your business," Mya replied.

"Anything concerning him is my business. Again why was she here?" I asked looking at Trent.

"She wanted me to help her out with her bills. I was just dismissing her ass when you walked in."

I was real skeptical about what he said. I was far from naïve and I knew there was more to the story but what's done in the dark will come to the light.

"Well bitch be gone," I said staring at her. She rolled her eyes but I didn't give a damn.

Mya walked passed me and smirked. I wanted to punch her in the damn face. Instead, I closed the door before she could make it all the way out causing her to trip, almost falling on her face. I turned my attention to Trent.

"I don't know what that was but don't fuck with me Trent. I will fuck you and that bitch up." I wasn't about to be dealing with that cheating shit. I mean I knew he's a man and all and I wasn't giving him any yet but damn, keep that shit in the streets. Again, I say, I shouldn't know about his extracurricular activities. Not saying I'm excusing him cheating but if he does, he needs to keep it out of my damn face.

"Chill ma. Ain't nobody fucking with that girl."

He stood up and walked over to me. I knew he was full of it I just didn't have the proof right now.

"I thought you were going to the mall with ya girls," he said trying to change the subject. I explained to him what happened and he was heated.

"So that nigga disrespected you?" he asked me, being sure of what I said.

"Yup and that bitch stood there like it wasn't a big deal. I know that's her nigga and all but she was supposed to be my girl. There's no way I would let that happen to her." I saw the little vein pop out in Trent's forehead and I knew that he was gonna confront Reggie.

"It's cool. Maybe you need to leave home girl alone because she seem like the type to leave you fighting in the streets. You don't need nobody like that around you." Trent kissed my lips and I immediately became hot. That had been happening a lot lately and I was leaning more towards giving him my virginity but I wasn't all the way sure.

He grabbed my plump ass and I felt my panties get moist. Lord help me because this man was breaking me down. He pulled away and left me there stuck. He went and sat back at his desk.

"So you kicking it with me for the rest of the day ma?" he asked as he shut his computer down.

"Yup." I walked over and sat on his lap. I was feeling horny and just wanted to be near him. I sat on his lap facing him. I bent down and kissed him. I parted his lips with my tongue and he accepted. We kissed and grinded on each other for a good five minutes. Yeah I was definitely ready and prom was on Saturday. I had a surprise for Trent.

When we finally came up for air he looked at me and said,

"Why you playing with me?" His dick was rock hard.

"I'm not playing. I just got caught up in the moment," I said as I got up off his lap.

"Keep playing I'ma put it on yo ass and you ain't gone be able to say shit," he said readjusting his pants.

"Is that a promise? I asked.

"Ma gone, cause you ain't even ready." He stood up and grabbed his coat and keys.

"Let's go." I followed him out of his office.

"Aye Brandon I'm out. Call me if you need me."
With that, we headed out.

*****

It was the night of my prom and because my daddy
didn't approve of me dating Trent, I told him that I
was going with the girls. I was with Chante getting
my hair and nails done. I still hadn't talked to Lashay
since that day Reggie disrespected me. That was
almost a month ago but hey, it is what it is. If she
wanted to holler at me then she could; but I definitely
wasn't calling her. I didn't do that fake shit.

"Girl I'm so geeked about prom." Chante was going
with Raheem. How the hell that happened I don't
know. Last time I checked he had a bitch at home. So
it was me, Trent, Chante, and Raheem riding together.
Trent had rented a Mercedes E-class limo. That boy
was bad as hell.

"Girl be careful. I know you feeling Rah, but he has a
girl." I didn't want to see my girl hurt.

"It's cool ma. He's just my prom date, that's it. I
know he got a bitch at home." Chante smiled at me.
Something told me that they had more going on than
she was letting on, but I'd eventually find out.

"Ok, I just don't want to see you hurt sis." Chante
was my girl and I wanted the best for her.

"Now back to you. Are you giving Trent the goodies tonight or what?" she asked changing the subject.

"That's the plan. I'm nervous though," I admitted. I had seen Trent's dick one day when he got out of the shower and that thing was huge. Being a virgin that shit made me scared to even try, but whenever I was around him, I was horny and ready. I decided it was time to put my big girl panties on.

"Girl don't be. Watch tomorrow yo ass gone be calling me bragging about yo night." We laughed. I was the only one from our clique that hadn't had sex, but that night was the night. We finished getting our hair and nails done, and then I dropped Chante off and headed home to get ready.

When I got home, my parents weren't home but there was a note. They were letting me know that they'd be there to see me off and that they loved me. I headed upstairs to shower and get ready. That night was definitely going to be a night to remember.

Chapter Three

Drunk in love

"Mom that's enough pictures we have to get going." My mom was snapping pictures like we were never coming back. I mean we did look good but damn. I was wearing a strapless aqua dress. It had a split right in the front that stopped just below my thigh. The top was beaded in rhinestones.

Chante's dress was similar but it was red. "Have fun ladies and be careful," my dad said before we headed out the door.

We hopped in my truck and headed to Trent's to meet the guys and get our night started. It took us about twenty minutes to get there and when we arrived, the limo was waiting. Trent walked up to my car and helped me out and Rah did the same for Chante.

"You look nice ma," He said, and then kissed my lips. Damn I loved those lips. They were big, not too big but big and juicy. I often day dreamed about what he could do with those lips.

"So do you bae." We headed to the limo and were on our way.

There was a nice turn out. We had our prom at Cobo Hall and it was live. We danced and talked shit all night long. Lashay even spoke to us. I wasn't petty, so I spoke, but I didn't think we would ever be as close. It was definitely a time to remember. Around one a.m. they wrapped it up. Everyone was headed either to a hotel room or to an after party. My baby had rented us a suite at the Marriott and I was ready.

We had the limo drop us off and Rah and Chante left. I assumed they were headed home.

"Ma I'm about to get in the shower. Why don't you find us something to watch on TV?" Little did he know TV was the last thing on my mind, if I had my way we'd be sexing all night long.

"Ok bae." While he was in the shower, I grabbed my bag. I was setting the mood with candles and all. I even bought lingerie. I had a black see through teddy with the nipples cut out and the crouch cut out. I had put that on with some black stilettos and pinned my hair up. When Trent walked out the room, I was sitting on the bed looking sexy. His mouth was wide open.

"Damn ma," was all he could say. I motioned for him to come to me and when he did, I pulled his towel away and my damn. He was working with a definite monster, I kind of bitched up. I guess he noticed the look on my face.

"No worries ma. I got you." He pushed me back on the bed and kissed me. He kissed me with so much passion. He took his time kissing every inch of my body. By the time he made it to my inner thighs, I was ready. He kissed each one of my thighs and then he inserted his finger in my pussy and pulled it back out. He tasted my juices and then he dived head first into my sweetness. Now that was the first time I was experiencing that kind of pleasure but I wished I had been did it. The pleasure I was receiving from Trent had me on cloud nine and we hadn't even had sex yet. He bit down on my clit, not hard but just enough that it felt good. Then he drove me off the cliff when he inserted his tongue inside my pussy. This man was tongue fucking me and before I knew it, I was shaking. Now being a virgin but smart, I assumed I had just had my first orgasm and I loved the feeling in every way.

For a good ten minutes, he feasted on my kitty like it was the last supper. My legs began to shake once more. That brought the total count for my orgasms to three. I didn't know what he was doing to me but it felt good and I never wanted it to end. If the sex was as good as his oral then I was about to be sprung.

"That's it ma. Cum all in my mouth." And that I did. As he came up for air, I lay there motionless. I had just experienced the best head ever. Well to me because that was my only experience. He climbed back up towards me and positioned himself between my legs. He looked me in the eyes and asked "Are you sure you're ready ma?" I just shook my head and he slowly penetrated me, stopping once the head was in. He looked at me once more and asked if I was sure.

"Yes," I replied as I looked in his eyes confirming my answer.

"Damn you sexy as hell ma." He eased in a little more I squirmed. It felt like he was ripping my insides apart.

"Don't tense up ma. Once it's in the pain will go away." I loosened up and he eased all the way in and just sat still. Then he slowly started rocking back and forth and the pain was replaced with pleasure.

"Damn baby your shit tight and fits my dick like a glove." He took his time with me and I was loving it. I felt that sensation in my body again. I had come once more. I didn't know it was humanly possible for someone to cum that many times.

"You love me A'more?" he asked as he looked at me, but it was feeling so damn good that I all I could do was nod my head yes. My words wouldn't come out. That man had me gone and it was only the first time.

*****

Trent

Damn. Little mama had that gushy and her shit was tight as fuck. That's all mine too. Last night was one of the best nights. I had no intention of sleeping with her yet. I was waiting for her to be ready, but she surprised the hell out me last night. And I think she got a little freak in her. She kept her stilettos on the whole time and that shit was sexy as fuck. I was

laying here watching her sleep. She was sexy as hell.
I didn't want to wake her because she looked so
peaceful, but checkout was at noon, and plus we were
meeting Raheem and Chante for breakfast. I didn't
know what's up with those two but hey.

"Ma wake up." She rolled over and smiled at me.

"Hey bae," she spoke. I pulled her in my arms and
kissed her. I was ready to go another round but I
wanted to let her body rest being that I had just broke
her in last night. But to my surprise, she climbed on
top of me butt ass naked.

"Teach me how to ride Trent." Damn she was sexy as
hell. I lifted her up a little so that I could slide in her
already wet pussy. The look of ecstasy on her face
made my dick harder than it already was. Damn I
think I was in love with her ass. I guided her hips in
the right rotation and after a short lesson; she was
riding me like she was a pro. I think I had an
undercover freak on my hands. We went at it for a
good fifteen minutes before we both released. I could
definitely get used to that.

"Get up and get dressed we're meeting Rah and
Chante for breakfast." She got up and headed to the
bathroom. While she was in there I grabbed her
birthday present from my gym bag. It was a 10-carat
diamond tennis bracelet. Her birthday was next week
but I wanted her to have it early. When she walked
out the bathroom, it was sitting on the nightstand.

"Come here ma." She walked over to me and I had to chuckle on the inside because she was walking as if she was sore. I must have torn that shit up last night and then she wanted more that morning.

"I know ya birthday ain't until next week but happy early birthday." I passed her the box and she opened it.

"Bae this shit is fly! Thanks so much." She kissed me. I had gotten her a Pandora bracelet and she had a heart charm because her name was A'more and in Italian, it meant "My love." She was definitely my love. The other one was a graduation cap because she was graduating soon.

"Here let me put it on for you." I helped her put it on and then we finished getting ready.

A'more

Trent is spoiling the hell out of me. I mean my daddy does too but Trent does things just because, and I love it. Plus last night was the bomb. I was officially addicted. We got dressed and headed to meet Rah and Chante at IHOP. I made a mental note to ask her about that.

When we arrived at IHOP Chante and Rah were already there. He was all up in her face like they were a couple. What made me mad was the fact that he had a girl but yet he was all up in my girl face. We sat down across from them.

"Hey sis. Hey Rah," I spoke as I looked over my menu.

"Hey lil' sis," Raheem spoke.

"Hey mama." Chante finally took her attention away from Rah to speak. Don't get me wrong, Rah is a nice guy but he has a chick and I think Chante is playing a dangerous game messing with him.

"So what's your plans for later?" I asked Chante.

"Sleep girl. I hardly got any last night so that's the plan." I shook my head at her. I knew her ass was with Rah all night. I gave her a look that said we were going to talk later. She just smirked. We kicked it for a couple of hours before we parted ways. Trent took me to my car and we made plans to hook up later.

Chante

I know you wondering how he hell I ended up going to prom and kicking it with Raheem. Well I ran into him a while back and we got to talking. Long story short, he got into it with his girl and called me to talk about it and we'd been kicking it since. That was damn near a month ago. We hadn't had sex or even dated. We just kick it from time to time. But the more time I spent with him the more I fell for him. I hadn't told him yet but I think he knew, because he would do little slick shit like smack me on the ass or wrestle. A lot of times, he would come over and spend the night with me but he always slept at the foot of my bed. I didn't want to cross the line because he had a girl, but as soon as they dead that shit he belongs to me; and that looks as if it will be soon.

I knew A'more was wondering what was up. I knew she has my best interest at heart. Now Lashay on the other hand has been acting hella shady lately. I hadn't even talked to her since her bitch as boyfriend pulled that disrespectful shit with A'more. I would never play my girl for a nigga. But some bitches ain't loyal.

I was lying in bed when my phone went off alerting me that I had a text message. It was from Raheem.

Rah: Wyd ma?

Me: Lying down. You?

Rah: just got into it with ol' girl. Can I come over? I need to get away.

Me: Yeah come on.

That was a normal routine for Rah and me. He would get into with his girl and then he'd come spend the night. It was cool because my mom wasn't here during the night. Plus she likes him anyway. They were like best damn friends. She worked third shift at the hospital so it was always just me here. I got up and brushed my teeth. I didn't want to be all up in his face with stink breath. Ten minutes later Rah was knocking. I headed to the door in just my boy shorts and tank top. When I opened the door, he was standing there looking good as ever. His eyes were low and he smelled like weed so I knew he was high. I stepped aside so that he could come in but he surprised me by hugging me. He damn near picked me up off the floor. I mean I only stood 5 feet even and he was at least 5'11. It felt damn good to be in his arms too. He let me go and walked inside.

"Come on, we can go to my room and chill," I said as I walked towards my room. He followed. I laid back on the bed and watched as he kicked his shoes and his pants off and laid down next to me. He pulled me towards him and asked, "Why we never hooked up Tae?" That was a question I never expected.

"Because you've always been with Michelle and I don't play second to no one."

"What if I told you that I'm no longer with her?" That was a shocker. For as long as I can remember, they had been a couple and to hear him say they were no more was music to my ears. That was my chance to get my man, but then again I didn't want to be a rebound chick either.

"I would say take it one day at a time and see what happens." He just pulled me close and kissed me. I had to be dreaming because for years, I had wanted that man and here he was in my bed kissing me. His hands traveled up my shirt and played with my nipples and that caused me to moan. Don't get me wrong I knew I should have stopped him but why? He was single and so was I, plus I wanted it just as much as he did. He flipped me over on my back and pulled my shirt off. He feasted on my breast like it was the last supper. That was my spot and my pussy was throbbing. Now I'm usually a person that likes to get head but at that moment, all I wanted was for him to fuck me good.

"Fuck me Rah." I gave him a seductive look that made him smile. He stood up and removed his boxers and that thing was huge. He was hung like a fucking horse. He snatched my panties off and started licking my kitty. Damn his tongue was lethal, and it didn't take long for me to cum. Before I knew it, he had climbed on top of me and entered me. Damn that shit felt good. As he pumped in and out of me, he whispered in my ear.

"I'm gone make you mines Tae. And I'll never fuck you, we make love." Did that nigga just say that shit? What was really going on?

Raheem

I always had a thing for Chante but I was with Michelle and it just was never the right time. But now that Michelle's ass was gone, I could snatch Tae ass up. I was the only one that called her that. The sex was the bomb and there was no way I was passing that up. Plus shorty was smart and wasn't a hood rat.

I left her house early that morning before her mom walked in. I didn't want to but hey, a nigga wasn't trying to beef with ma dukes.

I was chilling at the barbershop when Trent walked in. That was my boy from way back when. We had done it all together. From hustling on the block to owning a few businesses together. He was one of the realest niggas I knew.

"What's good man?" He gave me a fist pound when he came in.

"Ain't shit. Just stopped through to kick it with these niggas." I was looking at my phone. I had a text from Tae. She wanted to know what I was doing. I replied to the text.

"I just stopped through to grab some papers and I'm headed out," he said as he walked to his office. I was about to swoop Tae up. I wanted to chill with her for the day. I was digging the hell out of shorty. She was cool and easy to talk to. She was kind of like my best friend and soon to be lover.

"A'ight man I'm out. Hit me up later." He left and I texted Tae to let her know I was coming through.

*****

When I pulled up to Tae's house she was sitting on the porch kicking it with A'more. I was glad they weren't fucking with that bitch Lashay anymore. That broad was as grimy as they come.

"What's up lil' sis?" I said to A'more.

"Hey brother." I bent down and kissed Tae's cheek.

"What's up lil' mama?"

She smiled. "Hey Rah."

Damn that girl was fine as hell. I felt like a little bitch with butterflies all in my stomach. I sat down in between Tae's legs and pulled her arms around me.

"What the hell is this? Is it something y'all want to tell me?" A'more looked at both of us.

"Well I'm tryna snatch ya girl up but she playing," I said while kissing Tae's hands one after the other. We had a conversation that morning before I left about us making it official but she wasn't sure. She was playing games and shit.

"I'm not playing games but you did just break up with ol' girl and I'm not the rebound chick."

"I hear you ma. I'll show you better than I can tell you." I meant every word. Tae was special; she wasn't just a chick from the hood. She didn't fuck with a lot a dudes and she was as real as they come. We were chilling for a good minute when A'more announced she was about to meet up with Trent.

Those two were cute together. Hell, she was way better for my bro than that bitch Mya.

"So Tae can you get away tonight or is ma dukes gone be home?" I wanted to take her to my crib and just chill without having to leave early because her mom was coming home.

"Nah I can leave," she responded.

"Well go pack a bag and let's go." She looked at me.

"Where we going?" she asked me.

"Just go do it," I demanded. She went in the house to pack her bag and I went to my car and waited. She came back out a few minute later with an overnight bag and got in. damn she looked good in my passenger seat. I pulled off and headed to my crib to spend some time with shorty.

Chapter Four

So Into You

Trent

I didn't know what it was about A'more, but I was
digging shorty like crazy. I had been kicking it with
her for a few months now but hadn't seen much of
her because I had been mad busy with the
barbershops but she was that deal. I was looking for
my wife and so far, she has met the criteria. Yea she
was young but she was smart as hell and most
importantly, she wasn't no damn hood rat.

I was glad I was out of the game because she didn't
seem like the type to date a hustler. I did what I had to
do to get by but I turned that shit into something
positive. I wasn't trying to hustle forever like most
niggas do. I wanted more out of life. I was doing
pretty well though. I was 21 with a bachelors in
business administration and I had two barbershops
and a clothing store that I co-owned with Raheem.

I decided to text my shorty to see what was up.

Me: What's up ma?
    Wifey: Hey!

Me: What you doing today?

Wifey: Hanging with the Chante. Why what's up?

Me: I need to see you.

Wifey: ok when?

Me: Now

Wifey: lol. I'm at Chante's

Me: On my way

I hopped in the Charger and headed to Chante's
house. I needed to dig up in them guts. Since the first
time we did it a nigga been hooked. I wanted
whenever and wherever. I pulled up right behind my
baby's Mercedes. I knew her parents had money
cause she was riding nice as hell. I got out the car,
called A'more, and told her to come outside. A few
minutes later, she came out the door looking good as
hell. She was rocking some Levi's with a baby tee
that showed off her pierced belly and she had on the
Gamma blues. She was thugged out and cute at the
same time.

"What's up ma?" I asked as I pulled her into my
arms.

"Just chilling with the Chante and Rah and getting
ready for graduation," she responded as Rah came
outside.

"That's what's up. Well we out. Catch y'all later." I
gave Rah a fist pound and me and my shorty headed
to the car.

A'more

After I told Chante bye we headed to Trent's house in Canton. I loved his house. It wasn't huge like the one I lived in with my parents but it was cozy.

"Find us a movie ma," he told me as he headed upstairs. He came down five minutes later in basketball shorts and a beater. Damn that nigga was fine as hell. If he kept looking that damn good I was gonna say fuck the movie. I fought the urge to look at him but it was hard.

"I see you looking ma," he joked. I threw a couch pillow at him.

"Whatever." He sat down next to me and pulled me in his arms. I relaxed and laid my head against his chest. It felt nice. Too bad it wouldn't last long because I'd be leaving to go to Spellman in August.

"What you thinking about ma?" It was as if he knew something was wrong.

"About how I'll be leaving for ATL in a few months and I'm starting to like you."

"It'll work out. Stop worrying." That was better said than done.

*****

We had fallen asleep and when we woke up it was well after one in the morning. I jumped up in a panic. My parents were going to kill me.

"Trent get up!" I shook him awake.

"What's wrong ma?" he asked.

"My parents are going to kill me. It's after one in the morning. I need to get to my car." He stood up and grabbed his keys off the coffee table.

"Come on ma," he said as he headed to the door.

When we got in the car, I noticed I had a ton of missed calls from my mom and Lashay. Damn.

"My bad ma. I didn't mean to fall asleep but I was just so damn comfortable with you," Trent said.

"It's cool. I just hope my daddy isn't home." Twenty minutes later, we pulled up at Chante's house. I hopped in my car without even saying goodbye to Trent. On the way home, I called Chante to see if my mom had called her.

"Girl where the hell are you? Your dad is going fucking nuts looking for you."

"Fuck!" I hit the steering wheel. "I fell asleep at Trent's."

"Damn girl. Well your dad has been here looking for you," Chante informed me. I knew I was as good as dead.

"Alright girl. Let me get off this phone I'll call you later." I hung up before she could respond. It took me a good twenty minutes to get home. I looked at the time on the dash and it read 2:35. I got out the car and prepared to face the music. Every light was on in my house.

When I walked in my dad was sitting in the chair in the foyer like he was just waiting for me to walk through the door.

"Where the hell have you been?" He started on me as soon as I walked through the door.

"I was with a friend and I fell asleep. I'm sorry Daddy." I felt like I was five years old being scolded by my father.

"Try again. I called both of your friends and went by their houses. Your car was there but you weren't." He looked at me dead in my eyes. I looked to the right and my mother stood there helpless. I knew she wouldn't come to my defense because she always did whatever my father said. She didn't have a backbone.

"I told you where I was Daddy," I responded. I really didn't want to tell my daddy that I was with Trent because he had told me he didn't want me seeing him.

"Yeah, you were out being a slut."

"What!" I was shocked at my father's choice of words.

What's his name?" he asked me. I didn't respond.

"I asked you a question!" he yelled.

"Trent," I responded.

"Well you can just walk right back out of my door
and let Trent take care of you. Let him pay your
tuition cause as of right now you are no longer a part
of this family. Since you want to go against what I
said, then take care of yourself." I was stunned and
couldn't believe the words that had come out of my
father's mouth. For as long as I could remember I was
daddy's little girl, but standing here right now, I felt
like a stranger. My own father had disowned me.

"Mommy say something. I didn't do anything," I
cried out for my mother to help me but she never
came to my rescue. She just looked at me with
pleading eyes that said she was sorry. I felt defeated
as I turned to leave.

"Leave the car keys," my father stated before I
walked out the door. I dropped them in the candy dish
that sat on the stand next to the door and headed out
with no destination in mind.

I headed towards Telegraph rd. All I had on me was
my cell phone and my purse. I had about ten dollars
to my name. I didn't want to call Trent but I didn't
know who else to call. I was stranded in Bloomfield
Hills with nowhere to go. I swallowed my pride and
called Trent.

Trent

After I dropped shorty off I headed back home to chill. I was tired as hell but couldn't go back to sleep because she wasn't here. In that short amount of time, I had gotten comfortable with her next to me. It took me a good thirty minutes before I had finally drifted off to sleep, but was awakened by the ringing of my phone.

"Hello?" I didn't even bother to look at the screen.

"Trent, can you come get me please?" That voice woke me all the way up.

"Where you at ma?" I was confused because I thought she was home with her parents.

"I'm at the McDonald's by my house. My dad put me out and took my car."

"What the fuck yo! Tell me exactly where you at." She told me where she was and I headed out the door.

"I'm on my way ma. Just sit tight." I didn't know what kind of shit her pops was on but he was foul as hell for putting her out in the middle of the damn night.

It took me a good twenty minutes to get to baby girl because I was flying down 696. I was heated and was ready to pump some hot shit into her pops. He better be lucky he was her dad.

When I pulled up, I could see her through the front window. She was sitting at a table in the back. I headed inside to get her and take her home.

"Hey ma." She stood up and fell right into my arms.

"Thanks for coming. I didn't know who else to call," she cried.

"It's cool ma. I got you, believe that." I escorted her outside to my Range Rover and helped her in. Her response was a weak smile. I got in and we headed to my crib.

The whole ride there was silent except for a few sniffles here and there from A'more. When we pulled up to my crib, she just sat there staring out the window. I got out and walked over to the passenger side to let her out.

"Come on ma," I helped her out and to the door.

"Why don't you go get comfortable, and if you need something to wear just look in the drawer. I'll be in the den if you need me." I kissed her forehead and she headed upstairs.

I sat in the den and rolled a blunt. I needed something to calm my nerves. I wanted to fuck her pops up, but fuck it. I had shorty, as long as she stayed true then I was going to be there for her.

A good hour passed before I decided to go and check on shorty. When I got upstairs, she was sleeping so peacefully. I went to the guest bedroom so that she could have her space. Plus there was no way I could lay next to her and not want to touch her. That shit was going to be hard, but she was dealing with enough. I mean I had my little side pieces I still fucked with from time to time. But I knew that with A'more living there I was going to have to cut them short. I went to sleep that night thinking about her sexy ass.

Chante

I had to double check my phone when A'more called me. Her daddy put her out because she stayed out with Trent. Where they do that? That nigga was straight bugging. There had to be more to the story. I couldn't believe he would play his daughter like that because of one fuck up.

"Are you ok mama? You know you can stay here, my mom won't mind." I wished there was more I could do for my girl. It was a fucked up situation she was in.

"I'm good chica. I'm here with Trent for now but if it doesn't work out I'll be at your door," she joked. That's the A'more I knew; full of life and laughter.

"Ok, well tell Trent if he fucks up I'll kill his ass."
She laughed but I was so serious. A'more and Lashay
were my sisters and I loved their crazy asses till the
death of me. Too bad Lashay was on some funny shit
lately.

"Thanks for being there for me sis." She must not
have known. I was as loyal as they came and would
forever be in her corner.

"You know I got ya back." We said our goodbyes and
hung up. Trent was a real dude so I knew she was in
good hands.

▪▪

I woke up to a good morning text from Rah and that
made me smile. I texted him back.

Me: Good morning

Rah: WYD today?

Me: no plans as of yet

Rah: get dressed

Me: OK

I didn't know what he had planned but I didn't care.
All I knew was I was going. I got up and headed to
the shower. It only took me about ten minutes and
then I was out. I decided to keep it simple with black
Levi's and a blue baby doll tee. I wore my Gama
blues and pulled my hair up into a ponytail. Five
minutes later Rah was knocking.

"Hey," I said as I opened the door. He pulled me in his arms and kissed my neck.

"You look good ma." I smiled. I never got tired of his compliments.

"So where we going?" I asked as I put my coat on.

"You chilling with me today. Don't worry ma, you're in good hands." We headed to his Escalade and he helped me climbed in before heading to the driver's seat.

Rah drove for about thirty minutes and we pulled up to a nice crib out in Canton. It wasn't flashy but it was nice.

"Whose house is this?" I asked.

"Trent's."

I was hyped now because I could see my girl. Rah came over to the passenger side and opened the door for me. Nice.

When we got inside A'more was sitting watching TV and Trent was laid out across her lap.

"Aww, how cute."

She looked up and smiled. "Hey sis," she spoke.

"Hey mama. How you feeling?" I wanted to make sure she was ok.

"I'm good. I'm gonna call my daddy in a few days after he has calmed down."

"Ok, well you know I'm here if you need me mama."

"I know sis and I appreciate you." I knew she meant what she had said.

"I know boo, that's why I fuck with you." We all laughed and kicked it for the rest of the night.

Trent

I was lying next to my little mama watching her sleep. She looked so peaceful and innocent. Damn, in just a short amount of time she captured my heart. Something no other woman has ever done. I pulled her close to me and she smiled.

"Hey you," she said with her eyes still closed.

"How did you sleep ma?" I asked her as I kissed her neck. I inhaled her scent and she smelled like roses. Damn I was addicted to that girl.

"Like a baby. This bed is the shit bae." We laughed.

"What are your plans for today ma?" I asked. I wanted to chill with her but I had some shit to handle for her birthday and I didn't need her involved. I wanted her eighteenth birthday to be the shit. I was flying her and her girls to the Bahamas with the fellas and me. Since she was leaving for school soon I wanted to give her a birthday to remember.

"I didn't really have any plans. Besides I know Chante is laid up with Rah somewhere," he laughed.

"True. Well I have to go handle some business but I'll be back in a few." I kissed her luscious lips and that made my little friend jump. I was definitely getting some of that shit later.

"Ok, just hurry and come back to me." She got up and headed to the bathroom, ass jiggling and all. Damn she fine.

*****

I was in my office at the barbershop waiting on Chante and Rah. I needed her help pulling it off without A'more knowing anything. I looked at my watch and saw that they were twenty minutes late. Just as I was about to call them they walked in.

"About damn time."

Chante smiled. "Blame ya friend here. He plays too damn much." Rah just shook his head.

"Well let's get down to business. I want baby girl to have a ball and have no worries. We know that she's dealing with a lot from her parents so I want to cheer her up and this trip will no doubt do this. It'll actually give us all a piece of mind." We talked about the plan and dates and a good hour later everything was set. Chante told me A'more already had a passport because her parents traveled a lot, so that was a good thing. We decided to wait until after graduation to leave.

"Well then that's settled let's meet up later. I wanna party." Rah said.

"Cool we can chill at Club Skyy tonight." I needed to get out anyway. It had been a minute. We made plans to meet up later and they headed out.

Raheem

I'd been kicking it with Tae for a few weeks and we were taking it slow. I was feeling her. She was smart, sexy, and easy to talk to. Most of all she kept it real. Too bad, she wasn't fucking with a nigga like that though. She made it very clear that we were only friends with benefits. But I knew that eventually she'd be mine. Watch.

We were chilling in VIP at Skyy. It was Tay and me, Trent, A'more, Brandon, and his girl Shayla. It was packed damn near wall to wall. As usual though, we paid for a VIP section. We had blunts floating and bottles popping. It was just one of those nights where we kicked it and had fun. No worries.

I was sitting next to Tae and she was looking sexy as hell. I leaned over and whispered in her ear.

"You coming home with me tonight ma?" She looked at me and smiled.

"Nope. You are not my man." See, she be playing games and shit. We did everything that a couple did, even having sex, but she was playing games. Fuck it. She wanted to play; I was about to give her ass a show. I texted Michelle to see if I could slide through later. If Tae wanted to play that friend shit then fuck it. It is what it is. I didn't chase pussy. I don't know what the fuck she thought. I was about to head out. I needed some relief since Tae was playing with a nigga.

"I'm out y'all." I stood up and that got her attention but it was too damn late. I said my goodbyes and headed out before she could even respond.

Chante

I knew I was treading dangerously and I had to be careful with a nigga like Raheem. I was bound to get my heart broke. I knew that was what I'd always wanted, but now that I had a chance to have it, I wasn't so sure anymore. I knew he was mad but I had to look out for my best interest. I needed to know that he wanted me and that I wasn't just a rebound. I just hope that I didn't already mess it up.

We partied well into the wee hours and since I came with Raheem and he had already left, Trent took me home. I felt like a third wheel sitting in the back seat. Yeah I had to get my shit together fast.

"Alright y'all be safe," I said as I climbed out the
back seat and headed towards my door." Tonight
would be another lonely night. Usually Raheem came
by and stayed the night with me, holding me, or
sexing me, but for some reason I didn't think that was
one of those nights.

As I laid back on my bed, I thought about prom night.
I didn't have a date and he volunteered to take me.
We had a ball that night. We ended up getting a room
but he didn't try anything. He was the perfect
gentleman. We just slept in each other's arms all
night. I knew he had a girl but I also knew they were
damn near over. Lying in his arms just felt so right
and now I didn't know if I'd ever feel that again.

Raheem

I had just finished blowing Michelle's back out and it
was time to go. Don't get it twisted, we weren't
getting back together. I mean I had love for her but I
wasn't in love with her. Our relationship had run its
course. I was in love with someone else but they were
too damn selfish to see it.

The next day I found myself on Tae's block. I
couldn't get that girl out of my head. There was
something about her ass that had me gone and the
pussy was a plus. Damn, that was all bad. I knew she
was probably pissed at me for leaving her at the club,

but I had to get some air. She had me so far gone it didn't make sense.

I pulled up in front of her house and killed the engine. I texted her and told her to come open the door and she told me to go to hell. So I got out and knocked on the door. Her mom was still home and she liked me so I was good.

"Hey Raheem. How are you baby?" she asked when she opened the door.

"Hey ma." Yeah we were that cool that I called her ma.

"Chante's in her room. I'm headed to work but make sure you're out of my house by eleven. Don't make me hurt y'all."

"I got you ma. Be careful out there." She left out the door and I headed to Tae's room. I didn't even knock.

"Why are you here Rah? I'm not in the mood." I ignored her. took my pants off. and climbed in bed with her. She turned around and started running off at the mouth but I shut her ass up with a kiss. She resisted at first but then went with the flow. I finally let her up for air.

"Why are you fighting me so hard ma?" She looked at me in the eyes.

"Because I know you Rah and I'm not for the bullshit." I pulled her close to me.

"I would never do you wrong ma. For some reason I'm digging the hell out of you. I'm trying to see where this thing goes with us. Just fuck with a nigga and I promise I got you ma." She just snuggled up close to me and buried her head in my chest. Damn, I was gone get caught up fucking with her but I was addicted to her.

Chapter Five

Prettiest Girl

A'more

I never got tired of being under Trent. I mean we had our times where we did our own thing, but when it was us, it was us. We had grown close over the last couple of months. It was the day of my high school graduation. I was hoping my parent's showed up. I had called my mom a few days ago but she didn't answer. I even texted her, but no answer. If they didn't show up for one of the most important days in my life, then fuck it. I would officially be done with them. I had gone to the salon earlier and got my hair and nails done, so we just sat around chilling until it was time to go. I was nervous but excited. The day had finally come for me to enter into adulthood. I decided to stay home and go to school. At least I'd be near my girl and my man. Plus Wayne State had a good nursing program.

"So are you ready ma?" Trent asked. I was in the kitchen making a sandwich as he walked up to me and grabbed my waist. He planted small kisses on my neck.

"I am. I've been waiting for this day since forever," I laughed.

"Well before we go, I have a few surprises for you ma." He was always spoiling me with things. I mean my daddy did too, but it was different with Trent. He once told me he did the things he did for me because I was his Queen. He wanted me to look the best and have the best. I loved him for that. He was always making sure I didn't need anything and that I was satisfied before himself. He was a very selfless man.

"Awe bae you didn't have to get me anything. You do enough already." He kissed my neck again before letting go.

"You deserve any and everything I do for you bae. You complete me and as long as I have breath in me you will be taken care of." He pulled out a long jewelry box with a red bow on it and passed it to me. I opened it and my mouth dropped. It was a bracelet that had so many damn diamonds in it I was blinded. I was emotional because it was so thoughtful, and the bracelet was off the damn chain.

"Here is gift number two." That box was smaller. When I opened it, there was a car key inside. I know he didn't. I looked at him for confirmation and he smiled. I walked to the front door and I'd be damned. It was a 2014 silver Maserati. Just when I thought it couldn't get any better he passed me another box. That box contained a deed to a house in Bloomfield Hills. The deed had my name on it. The house sat on three acres. I was speechless.

"Ma I want you to have the best. You deserve it and I won't give you anything less. Congrats on your graduation ma." I kissed him and if we didn't have to leave, I would have fucked the shit out of him. That man was truly heaven sent and I would do everything I could to make him happy.

"Thank you so much bae, for everything you do for me. I love you."

"I love you too ma." The day was definitely starting out right. Nothing could spoil it.

*****

Trent

I loved it when I made her happy. She deserved it. There was more to come as long as she stayed down with a nigga and kept it real. It was crazy because the shit I did for her, no other woman has ever got that far with me. That's how I knew I was in love with her little ass.

Here we were sitting in the audience waiting to hear A'more and Chante's name. I was proud of them and now they both were headed off to college. They were lined up when I saw A'more looking around. I knew she was looking for her parent's but I didn't think they showed up and that was fucked up. You can't help who you fall in love with. It was crazy because her father was cut from the same cloth as me. We did the same shit. Only difference is, he still does that shit. Me on the other hand, I used it to my advantage. I invested my money. I also went to college. I knew I couldn't hustle forever. Shit a nigga like me too damn fly to go to jail.

"Amore Mancini!" The Principle called out and we got loud and ghetto cheering for my baby.

They called Chante's name and we did the same thing. When it was over, we met the girls outside with flowers.

"I'm so proud of you ma." She smiled but I could see the hurt. She wanted to share the day with her parent's but they never showed. Oh well.

Let's go celebrate y'all," I said. I knew it was going to be hell cheering her up but I was going to try my damnedest.

*****

It was time for our trip to the Bahamas. I told shorty we were leaving but she doesn't know where. All she knew is that it's a bunch of us going. It was 4am and our flight was due to leave at 6am. So I woke little mama up so that we could make our way to the airport and meet the rest of the crew.

"Bae wake up." She turned over and pushed my hands away. Yeah, we had a long night. I laughed when I thought about me blowing her back out. I made a mental note to talk to her about birth control even though I wouldn't mind her having my seeds, but we were still young.

"Ma come on, we have a flight to catch." She opened her eyes and looked at me.

"Really Trent." I knew she was irritated because she never called me by my name. It was always bae this and bae that.

"You can sleep on the plane ma. Now come on and get dressed." She threw the covers off of her and got up. She was ass naked and jiggling. Yes lawd she was blessed with a nice round ass and a set of perky D cups that I loved to suck and lick on. My dick was getting hard just thinking about it. I followed her to the shower because I was definitely about to hit that before we left. I couldn't help it, she was my addiction.

I stepped in the shower with her and pushed her forward. She knew the deal. With her ass tooted up, I entered her from the back and went to work.

Three hours later….

We were on our way to the Bahamas. When A'more finally found out, she was ecstatic. She had traveled with her parent's but never to the Bahamas. I knew she'd like it. I had been there a few times and it was nice as hell. I just wanted a nice vacation with my baby. I had already decided to let her meet my mom when we got back. I think it's time; no other chick I'd dated has met my mom, so that's big.

I looked over at A'more, my love and she was sleeping so peacefully. Raheem and Chante were right behind us and Brandon and Shayla were across from us. It was definitely going to be a trip to remember.

After our long ass flight, we finally made it to Nassau Paradise Island. I had set up an appointment for the ladies to go to the spa. I wanted them to be pampered and then we had a romantic dinner planned on the beach later that night. I was also hoping the trip would bring Rah and Chante closer. I knew they were feeling each other but they were playing games.

"After we get settled you all have a spa appointment. So go have fun, relax and maybe do a little shopping. Later on we'll have dinner and just chill."

"I'm cool with that because I need to relax. So let's go ladies." A'more kissed me and they headed out. It was just the fellas and me.

"So how are things going with you and Chante?" I asked Rah.

"Ok I guess. She's still hesitant to let me in and I can understand that, so I'm taking it slow. I'm crazy about her ass though. It's something about her that has me gone dawg. What the fuck yo." I had to laugh at that one.

"I know exactly how you feel because I'm crazy about A'more ass too. That girl is my other half. She holds a nigga down for real. No nagging and she takes care of home," I boasted on my baby.

"I feel that. Shay and I have been doing ok. I can honestly see myself with her long term" Brandon had been with Shayla almost as long as I'd been with A'more. They were close too. We all were in pretty good relationships and doing well on the business side. Things were good.

A'more

We had just gotten back from shopping. I loved the Bahamas. It was just too fucking beautiful.

"Hey fellas," I spoke as we walked through the door. Trent pulled me in his lap when I walked past him. He kissed me and I loved it. His kisses were sweet and addictive. I loved him and he was my drug of choice.

"Did you have fun ma?" he asked me.

"I did, thanks babe," she said handing me my Black card back.

"Nah that's all you bae. That way when you need something all you have to do is swipe ya card. If I got it like that then so do you." Damn that nigga was sexy.

"Well I'm going to go shower. What time is dinner?"
I asked and he told me seven, which gave me a good
hour and a half to get ready.

*****

Dinner was the bomb. We ate on the beach and it was
romantic. I never knew what Trent had up his sleeves.
He was always surprising me with new things and I
loved it. It was time to do something nice for him. So
when we got back I was going to start planning his
twenty-second birthday. I had a few months but I
wanted it to be the bomb.

Now as I lay in his arms I thought about how far I'd
come with him. I lost my family but I had gained a lot
more. My father turned his back on me and my
mother followed suite, but I'm doing good. Not that I
didn't miss them but that was their decision. It took a
minute but I fell asleep thinking about the day I
would become Mrs. Trent Davis. At least I hoped that
I'd make it that far. Who knew?

Trent

We had gotten back from the Bahamas yesterday and
I was taking A'more to meet my mom today. They
were the two most important women in my life and I
wanted them to know each other. A'more would be
the first woman that I let meet mom. That's how I
knew she was important.

Chapter Six

Lovers and Friends

Fast forward a year later...

Trent

It had been a little over a year since I met A'more and I'm happy to say shit is good. The barbershops are doing well and we didn't want for shit. I buy my baby shit just to say I did it. She just finished her first year at Wayne State. She didn't go away like she planned on but I'm glad she still stuck with school.

Rah and Chante are going strong. Weird because I never thought those two would hook up. Yup, her and my boy had made it official in the Bahamas last year and they've been rocking strong since. But they look cute together and they are even expecting a little girl in about three months.

I couldn't wait till the day A'more gave me a child. I was watching her cook breakfast in nothing but one of my t-shirts and I had the urge to go bend her over. Damn she was fine as hell.

"What you looking at boy?" she asked as she looked up from the stove. I walked over to her and kissed the back of her neck. That was her spot.

"Uh uh, we have things to do today for Chante's shower. I got you later." Damn a nigga was trying to get a quick nut.

"Come on ma. It'll be quick I promise."

"No Trent. Now let's eat so we can get our day started."

"Fine, but you owe me when we get home," I said as I sat down to eat.

"I got you bae." She smiled. That girl had my heart and she knew it. We finished breakfast and went to meet Rah to go over the details for Chante's baby shower.

*****

Everything was set for the shower and I was happy for them, but I was ready for it to be over so I could have my girl back. I was sitting in the den watching the game and blowing one when baby girl walked in butt ass naked. My damn eyes popped out of my head yo. That shit was sexy. She always did little spontaneous shit that kept our sex life popping.

"Damn ma it's like that?" She just smiled and got on her knees. She unbuckled my pants and pulled my dick out. Before I even knew what was going down she deep throated me and I couldn't even say shit. She had me squirming like a little bitch. I mean toes curling and everything.

I was nearing my peak and I tried to pull out because I would never disrespect A'more like that but she had a hold on me. I erupted and she swallowed every drop. Damn she was a bad bitch.

She stood up and straddled me. She didn't even let me take my pants all the way off before her pussy swallowed my dick. Her shit was tight as usual and I had to control myself.

"Damn ma, work that pussy. Shit!" She was riding the hell out of me. It didn't take long for me to reach my peak and I let go all up in her. I swear if she ain't already pregnant, she is now.

A'more

I had to keep it spicy because what I won't do, another bitch will. Not that me fucking him good will keep him from cheating but he'd never be able to say I didn't do my job. I keep him fed, fuck him good and I didn't nag him. A happy man means a happy household. Plus he deserved it. He kept me laced; he makes sure I'm happy so I do my job as wifey.

Today was my girl's shower and I was super excited for her. Soon my god baby would be here and I was going to spoil her rotten.

We had just finished setting up everything at our house for the shower and the guest had started to arrive. We were just waiting on Chante and Rah to get here and it was a go.

"You did a good job bae," Trent said kissing me on the cheek.

"Thanks bae." Then he whispered in my ear.

"When are you going to give me a little one?" I looked up at him like he was crazy. I wasn't ready for no kids.

"No time soon playa," I said as I walked away leaving him standing there.

Trent

A'more ass was playing games. I was serious and she was playing. I knew she was in school but she could have at least said when I'm done we'd talk about it. She just shut a nigga down quick. I took my ass over to a table and sat down. I was already done with the shower. I was ready for it to be over because I was officially in a sour ass mood.

Ten minutes later the shower had started and there were a lot of damn people there. They had so many damn gifts it was crazy.

"What up man? Why you over here?" Rah came over and kicked it with me.

"Ain't shit, I'm just chilling man. Congrats again man." I gave him a fist pound. We sat and chopped it up for a while until the shower died down. They had so much stuff that they had to leave some of it until tomorrow. All in all, it was a good day for them and I was happy for my boy.

I helped A'more clean up what the caterers didn't do and then we headed upstairs to call it a night. All I wanted to do was cuddle with the wife. Even though I was in my feelings earlier, I still wanted to be up under her. I loved her ass no matter what.

We climbed in bed and she snuggled up under me and fell asleep while I played in her hair. That was something her spoiled ass liked. She said it was relaxing. Soon after, I fell asleep.

I woke up to my cell phone ringing. It was five in the morning. What the hell. I looked over at A'more and she was out.

"Hello," I answered without even looking at the screen.

"Dawg get to DMC now! Shit is bad." That was Brandon. I didn't know what the hell was going on but I knew it wasn't good. I woke A'more up and told her where I was going. She insisted on coming with me and I didn't have the time to argue with her.

When we got to the hospital, I saw everyone but Rah. Then I looked in the corner and saw Chante in a fetal position crying and Shayla was trying to comfort her. What the hell was going on?

"What the fuck is this?" I asked. A'more had gone to Chante's side.

"Some niggas tried to rob Rah and shot him. He took two bullets. We don't know shit yet. We've been in this damn lobby for over an hour. We called you but yo phone just kept ringing until you finally picked up about thirty minutes ago." That shit was not happening. Not my boy. He had a baby on the way he needed to be here for.

"Family of Raheem Dunbar." The doctor came out and we all walked up to him. Before he could speak Rah's mother came walking in.

"Well Raheem took two bullets. One went into his chest cavity and came out his side. The other was still lodge near his spine. Now he's in a coma and we don't know how long he'll be like this. It is touch and go and right now it could go either way." That shit broke my heart. I actually let a tear fall.

"Are you ok ma?" I asked Rah's mother.

"Yes baby, it's in God's hands now. Why don't you all go home and get some rest and I'll keep you updated."

"That's a good idea. We'll take Chante with us." We all headed home. That shit was crazy. They were just happy and getting ready to welcome their baby in the world and now this shit. I took Chante home with A'more and me. She didn't need to be home by herself. We would visit Rah tomorrow and hopefully he'd be doing better.

*****

Two months later...

Chante

I sat in the chair next to Rah's bed. I was holding his hand and the tears were falling. We had become so close. Not only was he my fiancé but my best friend as well. Now here I was pregnant and alone. My daughter was due any day and my baby was fighting for his life because of some jealous ass person.

"Don't you think you should leave and let my son rest?" I turned to see Rah's mother Joy walk in the room. I swear that bitch was working my damn nerves.

"He is resting Joy. I'm just sitting here with him." I tried not to disrespect his mother but she was pushing my buttons.

"Look sweetie, what is it that you want from my son? His money?" No that broad didn't.

"Look Joy, I don't want nor need your son's money. What Raheem does for me, he does because he wants too. Don't come at me like that please. I guarantee it ain't what you want." I got up and walked out. I couldn't deal with the shit any longer. I needed for my man to wake up so shit could go back to normal.

Here I was, pregnant and alone. That was the time when I needed my girls, but A'more was dealing with her own issues and Lashay was being Lashay, as usual. We rarely spoke to her anymore. I headed home to take a nap because I was mentally and physically drained. Rah had been in a coma for almost two months now and I couldn't take that shit. I needed him; he was my rock, my best friend and my lover. Things had to get better because I couldn't take much more.

Trent

"Shit. Damn throw that shit back!" I couldn't believe I was hitting Mya I mean A'more has been acting real moody and stingy with the pussy. I ran into Mya and we kicked it for a minute. One thing led to another and here I was blowing her back out. I knew if A'more found out she'd kill me but I couldn't stop

"You like that shit daddy?" I wish the broad would shut the hell up. I was trying to bust a nut.

"Shut up and take this dick." I was nearing my point and she wanted to talk like I was making love. Bitch please I only make love to one person.

"Shit I'm about to cum." I let go and pulled out. I headed to the bathroom to flush the condom. After I flushed the condom, I headed back in the room to get dressed so I could be out.

"Damn, so just fuck me and leave huh?" That chick had the game all fucked up.

"You knew the deal ma," I said as I grabbed my keys and headed out the door.

"Fuck you Trent!" I already did I thought.

When I got home, A'more was asleep. It was early as hell and she was out. I didn't want to disturb her so I headed to the basement to chill. The game was on and I wanted to see these sorry ass Lions get whooped. It's a damn shame they can never win.

My face turned into a smile and I felt like shit when I got downstairs. My baby always thought about me and here I was out cheating. She had a blunt rolled for me and the game already on. I swear I was making that girl my wife. She had a little mouth on her but she took care of a nigga. Always had a hot meal to come home too and she used to give a nigga unlimited pussy but lately that hadn't been happening. I just charged it to PMS.

An hour after I came home my baby joined me downstairs.

"Hey ma. How did you sleep?" I asked her.

"Good. What you got up today?" she asked as she sat down next to me.

"Just chilling with you. I went to see Rah today and he's still the same. Chante's up there now." I pulled her on my lap. I felt dirty as hell because I had just come from fucking Mya and now I was cuddled up with wifey. What kind of nigga was I? Did I even deserve her? I knew if she ever found out it was a wrap for us. Damn.

*****

A'more

I was lying in bed when Trent's phone went off. I ignored it because it wasn't anything for me to be concerned with. He had been gone all day and headed straight to the shower when he got in. his phone went off again. Whoever it was was trying hard to reach him. Woman's intuition told me to look at the screen, so I did. There were three text messages from Mya. I was boiling. Why was he texting back and forth with that bitch? I opened the text.

Mya: What time are you coming? I need you daddy

Trent: I told you I was with my girl so chill.

Mya: Fuck that bitch. You weren't thinking about her the other night when you were all up in this pussy.

I didn't even read anymore. I tried everything in me not to let the tears fall. I had gone against my daddy's wishes to be with him and here he was fucking his ex.

He couldn't even keep that shit away from home. I heard the shower turn off and I wiped my tears. As soon as he opened the door, I threw the phone at his head.

"What the fuck is wrong with you?" I got up in his face.

"So you fucking that rat bitch huh? Was it good? Huh?" I mushed him in the side of his head. He stood there like a deer caught in headlights.

"Baby it's not what you think." I wasn't trying to hear it. That was the same shit all niggas said when they got caught up.

"Fuck you Trent." I grabbed my keys and headed out the door. He couldn't come after me because all he had was a towel wrapped around him. I drove with no destination in mind. Times like that I needed my mom. I knew I could talk to Chante but she was probably up at the hospital with Rah. I ended up at the Marriott. I had a lot to think about. Mainly the fact that I just found out I was pregnant. I had mixed emotions about it because I was still in my first year of college.

I checked in and headed to my room. My phone had been blowing up with texts and calls from Trent but I wasn't fucking with his ass. I texted Chante to let her know I was good because I knew he'd be calling her next and I didn't want her to worry.

After texting Chante, I undressed and got comfortable on the bed. I didn't know how long I was going to be there but I knew I needed a break.

Trent

I couldn't believe that shit was happening. Things weren't supposed to be like that. A'more was my shorty, my heart. I had to fix it, but how? I knew I was wrong for sleeping with Mya. It was one of those in the moment type things and shit just happened.

I texted A'more to see where she was.

Me: Where u at?

Wife: Fuck off

Me: Come on ma. I'm sorry

No response. Fuck. There wasn't really shit I could do now, so I just went to bed. I had a long day ahead of me tomorrow and I needed a clear head. I would deal with A'more later.

*****

When I woke up I checked my phone for messages for A'more but there was none. Fuck it. I got up and showered; it was time to get my day started.

I threw on some Black True's a white tee and some black Prada's. I had to meet up with Brandon and do some paper work. We were scouting out a new location to expand our barbershop. Business was booming and money was flowing.

When I pulled up to Brandon's house, I blew the horn for him to come out but he didn't come out alone. Chante was with him. She had been staying here and at our house since Rah's been in the hospital. A'more probably called her.

"What's up Chante?" I nodded.

"Hey Trent. Um have you talked to A'more today?" she asked.

"Nah, she isn't answering my calls or texts," I responded.

"Well I talked to her this morning. I don't really know what's going on between y'all and it isn't any of my business but she needs you. It's not my place to tell you but I'm going to be a friend and tell you anyway. She's pregnant." That whole revelation just blew my mind. How the hell did I miss that shit? That's why she's been so damn moody lately. And my dumb ass fucked up.

"Trent are you listening to me?" I was zoned the hell out.

"Huh? Oh yeah, I'm going to find her and talk to her. Thanks Chante'

During the entire meeting, I couldn't focus. All I could think about was A'more being pregnant. And I would hurt her by cheating when she needed me the most. I was happy as hell but then again I didn't know where we stood. I had fucked up royally and it was going to take a lot of ass kissing to get back good with her.

"Trent are you ok man?" Brandon brought me out of my thoughts.

"My bad dawg. I got a lot on the brain. Can we reschedule this meeting?" I needed to find my shorty and fix that shit.

Yeah that's cool man. Go handle yo business and hit me when you're done." I stood up to leave. I needed to bring my shorty home.

A'more

I had spent one night at the hotel and I already was missing my bed. It was time to go home. Plus I knew I couldn't stay gone too long. When I pulled up Trent's truck was parked in the driveway. I prepared myself mentally to deal with the issues we had. I killed the engine and just sat there for a minute collecting my thoughts.

When I finally went inside Trent was on the couch sleep. He had stress lines popping out of his forehead and I knew it was because of our situation. I walked right past him and headed upstairs to shower.

I adjusted the temperature so that it was just right before stepping in. I let the water hit my face and I felt relaxed. A few minutes later I felt a pair of hands wrap around my waist. I really didn't know how to react because truth was I loved the man with everything in me.

The tears fell from my face and I couldn't stop them. I was hurt but I was also in love.

"It's ok ma." He kissed my neck and just held me in his arms. He turned me around and kissed the tears as they fell. He went back to my neck. Damn him, he knew that was my spot. It made me weak. He brought his right hand down over my pussy and rubbed it. Instantly I was wet. It was like my body reacted to his touch. There was something about that man that had me addicted. Yeah I was addicted to love.

He started kissing me. First slow pecks but I couldn't take it anymore. I damn near assaulted his tongue. He lifted me up in one swift motion and brought me down on his throbbing dick. I gasped at the thickness. Even though we had made love countless times, I still never got used to the size of his dick. Every time was like the first time. It was pain mixed with pleasure. He was pumping in and out of me and I was in heaven.

"Fuck! Damn bae that shit feels good," I cried out.

"You like that shit ma?" I didn't answer.

"You hear me?" he pumped harder.

"Oh shit! Yes daddy!"

"Cum on this dick ma." That was all it took. I started leaking like a faucet.

"I'm cumming!"

"Me too ma," he grunted and let go.

That was probably the best orgasm I'd ever experienced. I slid down off of him and he washed me up and then himself. After he dried me off, he told me to lay across the bed and he lotioned my body from head to toe. That shit was so relaxing. That's what I loved about him. He always took care of me and made sure I was straight. We just needed to get past that issue and we'd be fine. Hopefully.

Trent

A'more was lying on my chest and I was playing in her hair. I loved shit like that. I could never lay like that with another chick. She was definitely my wifey.

"You want to talk about it ma?" I asked her.

"Nah. I just want to enjoy this moment for a minute." Her face said something different and I could hear it in her voice. I had hurt her. Damn. I knew shit would never be the same between us.

"Well tell me one thing." She looked up at me.

"Are you carrying my seed?"

"Yeah." She sounded disappointed. I didn't know if it was because she was disappointed because it was by me or the fact that she was still young.

"You don't sound too happy ma." She stayed quiet.

"Look at me ma." I pulled her face towards mine. "I told you I got you no matter what. You won't go through this alone. I love the hell out of yo ass. You are my A'more, my love." Her name was perfect. A'more was Italian for my love and that's what she was, my love. I would go through hell and high water for her ass.

"I hear you talking Trent but we'll see." Damn that hurt to hear my shorty question my love for her. I knew I had no one to blame but myself, but damn. I had to fix that shit.

A'more

As I lay in Trent's arms, the tears fell. I was torn between leaving him and staying. I loved him but I didn't know if I could deal with the bullshit. Only time would tell if we would make it.

I heard him snoring and I just laid there silently crying to myself. I felt lonely. My girl was dealing with Rah being in a coma and my man was cheating. I was supposed to be happy because we were expecting our first child but instead we were dealing with infidelity. That was the time when I needed my parents but they had disowned me all because of who I loved. Damn, did I make a mistake?

*****

I woke up to the smell of food and Trent's side of the bed was empty. The smell turned my stomach and I jumped right out of bed heading straight for the bathroom. I was bent over the toilet for a good five minutes. The bad part was, I hadn't ate yet so there was yellow stuff coming up and it hurt my stomach like hell.

"You ok ma?" Trent walked in the bathroom, sat on the tub beside me, and started rubbing my back.

"Yeah I'm good. I just need to brush my teeth and I'll be out." I really didn't want him anywhere near me. Every time he opened his mouth, I pictured him with that bitch Mya. I wanted to drag her ass up and down the fucking street. I brushed my teeth and washed my face then headed back to bed. Today was one of those days where I didn't want to do anything.

"I'll go make you some soup and get you some ginger ale and crackers." He was all of a sudden being attentive. Why couldn't he have done that shit in the first place? Had he been paying attention instead of fucking the next bitch he would have known something was wrong with me.

"Look ma I know I fucked up but I'm here for you. I'm sorry about that shit and I know it won't change the fact that I fucked up, but I am sorry." Yeah, yeah,

yeah, the famous line of a cheater. I didn't respond. I just wanted to sleep. Hopefully when I woke up that shit would all be a dream. Somehow, I knew that was a far stretch.

Chante

I was sitting at home when Trent called me to let me know Rah was woke and asking for me. I couldn't have been happier. I had been going through it these last few weeks. His mama was being a bitch and had stopped me from visiting him and because we weren't married I t was nothing I could do. I was due any day and Trent didn't want me driving so he was on his way to get me.

I was already dressed and waiting on the porch when Trent pulled up.

"Damn ma you were ready huh?" he joked.

"Hell yeah. I miss my man. Where's A'more?" she asked.

At home. She isn't feeling well." Aww my poor sis. I was going to have to hang out with her soon. We headed to the hospital and when we pulled up, I became nervous. Why I didn't know. I thought about when we first got together and how close we were. I thought about how I almost lost him because I was too damn stupid to realize he was the one for me. Fast forward and we were about to have a baby girl and were happy until someone tried to take him from me.

"Are you going to be ok?" I looked at Trent.

"Yeah. I've been waiting for him to wake up. I don't know what I would have done if I had lost him Trent." I was becoming emotional. It was a mixture of hormones and the thought of almost losing him.

"It's ok sis. Go on up and call me when you're ready to go."

"Thanks Trent." I got out of the car and headed in the hospital.

When I opened the door to his room, I almost broke down. My emotions were all over the place. To see him sitting up watching TV and looking as if nothing had happened to him felt good. I remember thinking he wasn't going to wake up but things changed for the better. I walked in the room and Rah looked up and smiled.

"Hey ma. Come here." He patted the bed next to him and I went and sat next to him. He pulled me in his arms and the tears began to fall. I had loved him since I was twelve and the thought of losing him was something I couldn't bear.

"Don't cry ma, I'm here." He rubbed my back and tried to console me.

"Baby I thought I was going to lose you," I cried more.

"I'm here ma and I ain't going nowhere." He rubbed my huge belly and our daughter kicked. I never imagined that I'd be here with that man, pregnant and engaged. He truly had me addicted to love.

*****

Amore

I was in bed when my phone went off. It was Chante.

"Hello?"

"Sis I'm in labor and I'm home alone. I just left Rah and then this shit happens." Shit!

"Hold tight baby I'm on my way." It's a good thing we only lived ten minutes away from her. I got up and threw on some sweats and gym shoes. I was going to tell Trent to come on but he wasn't home, strange being that it was 2 a.m. I would deal with his ass later right now, my sis needed me.

It only took me five minutes to get to Chante's being that my ass was running through stop signs. I had a key to her crib so I went right in and he was on the couch in apparent pain.

"Come on mama let's go have this baby." I helped her to the car with her stopping every few steps with a contraction. My niece was ready to enter the world.

Rah was still in the hospital so I recorded the whole thing. I even cut the cord. Armani Nicole Dunbar. She weighed 7 lbs. 8 ounces and looked just like Rah's ass.

"Thanks sis for being here," she said as she was dosing off.

"You know I got you till the world blow. Now let me go call Trent." I walked out in the hallway to see where the hell Trent was. No answer. That nigga was working my last damn nerve. I decided to go to DMC to visit Rah so he could at least see the video. I knew he was about to be pissed that he missed the birth of his daughter but at least he would get to raise her. I peeked in the room and Chante was sleep so I headed over the see Rah.

Trent

A'more had been blowing me up but I couldn't even talk to her right then. I had fucked up and when she found out it was over for sure. I hadn't cheated on her anymore but Mya was talking about she was pregnant. What the fuck was I gone do. Wifey was pregnant and now the side bitch.

Now here I was sitting at the bar getting fucked up. I had to fix that shit. I looked at my watch and it read 10 p.m. it was time to go home.

When I got home, A'more wasn't there. For once, I wasn't even tripping because I didn't want her asking me a bunch of questions. Just as I was lying down, my phone went off. It was A'more.

"Hello?" I decided to answer.

"Well damn, about time you answered the phone. Where the hell have you been?"

"I was out having a few drinks. What's up?"

"Well I was trying to call you and let you know that Chante had the baby. I'm here at the hospital with her now." Aw damn, I missed it.

"Alright I'll be up there in the morning."

"Alright. I already went by to see Rah and show him the video so I'm on my home now."

"Be careful ma," I told her

I decided I was going to be upfront with her. I didn't want any secrets between us. Whatever happened, fuck it. I jumped in the shower and prepared myself for the war. When I got out, I rolled a blunt and took a shot. I didn't know what A'more's reaction was going to be when I told her that Mya was pregnant.

"Hey bae." I didn't even hear her come in the door. Damn I was slipping.

"What's up ma?" She sat down next to me and I pulled her in my arms. She smiled that perfect smile that attracted me to her. I loved that woman with everything in me. I planned on marrying her one day.

"We need to talk about some things. I know I fucked up when I cheated on you with Mya and I'm dealing with the fact that I hurt you every day I love the hell out of you ma." She had a look on her face that I didn't like.

"You're scaring me Trent."

"Mya's pregnant but I don't think it's mine" Smack!

"You fucked her right? So how can you be so fucking sure that it's not yours?" I tried to hug her but she pushed me away

"Please baby don't do this. I'm so fucking sorry. I need you ma." She pushed me away from her and looked at me like I disgusted her.

"You don't need me. You said fuck me the minute you slept with her. Get the hell away from me." She got up and walked away and I didn't know what to do. I was losing my shorty and it was all my fault.

Chapter Seven

I Miss You

Trent

It had been a few weeks since A'more found out about Mya being pregnant, and things still hadn't gone back to normal. I couldn't blame anyone but myself. I had a bad bitch at home and I went elsewhere. I had left the house early that morning to go and get her a gift. I knew gifts wouldn't change the fact of what happened but I was trying to make it right. Hell, I still didn't know if Mya was pregnant by me or not. I hoped like hell she wasn't

When I got home, her car wasn't there so I assumed she was with Chante. At least she was getting out the house and not mopping. Well at least that's what I thought until I went upstairs and saw her clothes gone. I panicked. She had actually left a nigga. I dialed her cell phone only to be sent to voicemail. Two minutes later a text came through from her.

Wifey: I'm sorry Trent. I had to do this for me. The longer I stayed in that house the more I thought about you and her. I need some time to myself to figure out if I want to work this out or leave you for good. Don't worry I am keeping the baby and you will be a part of everything. I just didn't know if we'd be together.

I threw my phone at the wall and it shattered into pieces. I couldn't believe she had left a nigga. My heart was aching. I now knew how she felt when I cheated on her. I felt like shit but it was my fault and now I might have lost her for good.

*****

It had been two weeks since I'd seen A'more. She texted me every other day and let me know that she was ok. Today she sent a text telling me she had an appointment to find out the sex of the baby. I was getting ready to meet her at the doctor in a few.

When I pulled up to the doctor's office, her car was already there. I went inside and there she was reading a magazine. My heart sped up at the site of her, I was like a teenager. Man I hoped she came home soon.

"Hey ma." I sat down next to her and she smiled. At least I got that.

"Hey," she spoke. I reached over and rubbed her little pouch. She was four months but not really big.

"So we find out what we're having huh?" I was trying to make small conversation.

"Yeah. I hope it's a boy. What about you?" she asked me.

"I don't really care as long as it's healthy. But if I had to choose, I'd go with a girl that had your looks." I smiled at her.

"A'more Mancini," the nurse called. We followed the nurse back to a room where they gave her gown to change into. We waited for awhile before the doctor came in. A nigga was happy as hell.

"Good afternoon. Are we ready to see the baby?" the doctor asked when he walked in.

"Yes." I answered for both of us.

The doctor poured a blue gel on her stomach and began the sonogram. I didn't know what the hell I was looking at but I knew it was my seed.

"It looks like this one is a boy. There's his little penis." She pointed to the screen and my heart filled with pride. That's was my son.

"Ok the heartbeat is strong and he is growing just fine. We will see you all back in a month. You will do your sugar test and some blood work then. Until then, make sure you are drinking enough fluids especially water and try to eat healthy. If you have any questions feel free to call the office."

"Thanks doc." She left the room and I helped A'more get dressed. I was trying to get on her good side. Call it ass kissing or whatever but I missed my shorty and I was ready for her to come home.

"Thanks." She smiled at me. That was a start right?" We headed out of the clinic. I walked her to her car. I wanted to ask her where she was staying but I didn't want to overstep my boundaries; especially when I didn't know where we stood.

"So what are you about to do?" she asked.

"Go to the crib and chill. What about you?" I was trying to hold her as long as possible.

"Probably grab a bite to eat and then head home." Home. Damn I thought her home was with me. I knew it was over now. That was my chance to at least try and mend things with my shorty.

"Can I take you to lunch?" She looked at me like she was debating.

"Nah, but you can cook for me. Come on, I'll follow you because I'm starving." Damn that was easy. I opened her door for her and helped her in before going to my ride. We headed to the home I once shared with my baby.

A'more

I was sitting in our living room watching TV while Trent cooked for me. Yeah, I said our Living room. I wasn't ready to come home yet because I knew we needed our space, but I had planned on going back soon. I had to let him know that I wasn't going to tolerate his shit. Once a nigga cheat and you go right back to him, then he takes that at his cue to keep doing the bullshit. I loved Trent but I loved myself more.

I bet he thought I was staying that night. Wrong. I was going back to my hotel where I had been staying for the last few weeks. The only person who knew where I was staying was Chante.

"Here you go ma." He fixed me a grilled chicken salad and apple juice. I was about to tear that shit up.

"Thanks Trent." He looked at me with a puppy dog face. I never called him by his name. It was always bae, so he knew things weren't back right yet.

"You're welcome." We sat in silence while I ate and watched TV.

*****

We were watching "The Best Man" and Trent was rubbing my feet when his phone went off. He had a text. I tried to pay it no mind but that was hard to do. He looked at it but didn't open the text. He slid it in his pocket. Sneaky muthafucka. He wanted to keep playing huh?

"Well it's getting late so I'm going to head out." He got that sad look on his face again.

"It's too late for you to be driving ma. You can sleep in our room. I'll stay in the guest room."

"I don't think that's a good idea Trent." He was wearing me down. I wanted to stay but I knew I shouldn't.

"I just don't think that's a good idea Trent. I'll be fine and I'll call you when I get home," I replied trying to get up. But he stopped me.

"Come on ma don't make me take ya keys. I wouldn't be able to live with myself if I let you walk out that door and something happened. You can leave first thing in the morning." He got me.

"Fine." He looked relived. Plus I didn't feel like fighting with him. I knew he would definitely take my keys.

"Thanks ma. I just wanna make sure you and my son are ok."

"Thanks." We sat and watched the rest of the movie before we headed up to bed, me in the master bedroom and him in the guest room.

Mya

That nigga wanted to play games with me because that bitch was over his house. Well I was about to show his ass that I wasn't the one. I texted him and called only to be sent to voicemail. When I rode past his house, her car was there. I guessed they were back together, but not for long. Watch me work my magic. That bitch would be out of our lives if it was the last thing I did. That baby she was carrying had to go too. My baby would be the only one carrying his last name if I could help it. I made a call to my cousin

Marvin who was A'more's ex. Yeah, small world huh. Well I had a few tricks up my sleeve.

"Hey Marvin we need to talk about ya girl."

"What's the deal cuz?" he asked.

"Well you know I'm pregnant my Trent and now so is this bitch. I need her away from my man. She doesn't deserve him. Plus this is your chance for payback. We can get Trent to leave her alone for good. Now it'll take a minute for our plan to work but I'm willing to do whatever is needed to have Trent."

Chapter Eight

Stay and fight

Trent

It had been about two weeks since A'more had come over to the house. She still playing games so fuck it. I wasn't about to kiss her ass, if she wanted to be by herself then she could. I was doing me from now on. If it wasn't about my son then fuck her.

I had met a shorty about a week ago and today we were hanging out. She was bad too. Little red bone, 5'9", and she rocked a short bob. She had a nice little ass and she was a lawyer. I could definitely see myself chilling with her. Her name was Tangela.

I was looking nice today. It was a new day and I was getting over A'more's spoiled ass. I was rocking Marc Jacobs's cargo shorts and a white tee. Fresh air ones out the box. A nigga had just got a fresh haircut so I was looking nice. Tangela had invited me over to her crib for lunch and I was running behind. I grabbed my keys and cell phone and was out the door.

It was a nice day out. Ninety degrees to be exact. So I decided to drive my 2015 Mustang GT. It was candy apple red and shining. I had a thing for cars.

When I pulled up to Tangela's house, I was impressed. She lived in a nice neighborhood and had a nice house. I headed to the door and she opened it before I could even knock.

"About time. I was starting to think you stood me up." She smiled.

"Never that ma." I took her in my arms. Damn she felt good. She stepped back and let me in.

"It smells good in here. What did you cook?" I asked as I followed her to the kitchen.

"Spaghetti and garlic bread. Something simple." She turned around to be met by my lips.

I grabbed her in my arms and she wrapped her arms around my neck. Damn her lips were nice. Fuck the food.

I backed her up to the counter and lifted her up. She had on these little ass shorts that I slid to the side. While still kissing her I slid a finger in her wet pussy. Her shit was dripping. I stopped kissing her briefly to snatch her shorts and thong off. I unbuckled my pants and pulled my dick out. Yeah it was about to go down.

I pulled her to the edge of the counter so I could get better access and I went in. Damn her shit was tight. I couldn't even contain myself. My dick had a mind of its own. I fucked her so damn good we never even ate. She ended up going to bed and I was right next to her waiting for round two.

A'more

I had been texting Trent all day. No response. I was ready to go home. Shit, I call myself teaching him a lesson but that just made me miss him even more. I decided to pack all my stuff and head to the house. I could talk to him whenever he got home.

It took me a good hour to gather all my stuff and put it in my car. I moved a little slow being that I was five months pregnant. That little boy was making me tired as ever. When I pulled up Trent's Mustang was gone so I knew he was out and about. I just left my stuff in the car. I could have him get it later.

I hadn't been here in almost a month and that was the day of my last doctor's appointment. I went upstairs, changed into some pajamas, and waited in the den for Trent to get home. I decided I could watch a movie and order a pizza.

I must have fallen asleep because I woke up to the sound of voices. I sat up and I'd be damn. I heard a female voice. I know he didn't. In walked Trent and some light skinned chick. He didn't even notice me. I cleared my throat.

■■

"A'more, what are you doing here?" Did he, nah he didn't just ask me that.

"Uh my name is on the fucking deed! Or did you forget?"

"I mean you did leave ma. Come on let's be real. I've been trying to get ya ass to come home for how long?" The tears were threatening to fall. We separated for a minute because he was cheating and he moved on that quick.

"You know what, it's cool. I'm out." I stood up and headed to the door. I didn't even care that I had pajamas on. I was officially done with his ass. Here I am ready to get over his cheating and he has a new bitch already. It was cool. At least I knew where we stood with each other.

Trent

Damn. Could shit get any worse? I mean she left me. It wasn't the other way around.

"Um do you want me to come back another time?" Tangela asked.

"Nah ma you good. That was my ex and baby mama. We broke up almost two month ago and I guess she was ready to work it out, but it's too late." I didn't know if I was trying to convince her or me.

"Well I don't know what the deal is with you and her but that's not my concern. I'm here for as long as you need me to be." I liked the sound of that but did I really want to be done with A'more?"

"Thanks ma."

Chapter Nine

You Used to Love Me

Four months later….

Trent

Even though things didn't work out for A'more and me, I still miss her ass. I'm still kicking it with Tangela but she's just a distraction. I care about her but I'm in love with A'more. She's now due any day to have our son. We speak but it's always short.

"So what's the plan for today?" Tangela asked me. We were chilling in the den watching TV and she was lying across my lap the way A'more used to. Damn I had it bad.

"Well I have to meet with Rah and Brandon but after that I'm all yours ma." I was going over Rah's for a cookout but I wasn't taking Tangela because I had too much respect to bring a chick up in A'more's face. We weren't together but she was the mother of my child.

"Oh that's cool; I was kicking it with Cherise today anyway." Cherise was her ghetto ass friend. That bitch was always mean mugging me and talking shit. I had to check her ass one day. After that, I told Tangela not to bring her around me.

"That's what's up. You staying at yo house tonight?"
I was starting to feel smothered by Tangela. It was
like she always wanted to be up under me and I
wasn't feeling that. It just wasn't the same as having
my ex up under me. I guess you can say I was
addicted to A'more and probably would compare
anyone I dated to her.

*****

When I pulled up to Rah's house, I could see the
smoke coming from the backyard and the smell of
barbecue invaded my nostrils. I made my way to the
backyard where everyone was waiting. The first
person that caught my eye was A'more and her big
belly. She was glowing, Pregnancy really did agree
with her. I walked over to her and spoke.

"What's up baby mama?" I bent down and kissed her
cheek.

"Hey." She smiled.

"Aww y'all so cute." Chante joked. She was holding
my Goddaughter who was spoiled as hell. I walked
over to her and grabbed Armani from her.

"So where is ya girl at?" A'more asked trying to be
funny.

"She sitting right here with jokes," I challenged. She
rolled her eyes.

"Whatever." She went back to playing on her phone.
Yeah she was still playing games. I sat and played

with Armani and acted as if A'more wasn't even there.

"Ouch!" I looked up at A'more and she was holding her stomach.

"You good ma?" I put Armani down and went to her side.

"I'm good: I just had a sharp pain, probably from the way I was sitting." I wasn't buying that. She was due any day and I was worried.

"Ouch!" There she went again.

"Come on let's go." I was taking her to the hospital whether she wanted to go or not. I wasn't taking any chances. She stood up and then she peed on herself. What the fuck!"

"I think my water just broke." She looked up at me. Aww shit! That meant my son was ready to make his debut into the world.

"Y'all go ahead and we'll meet you there," Rah told us as we headed to my car. I helped A'more in the seat and then made my way to the driver's side. Damn I was about to be a father.

Three hours later Christian Dior Davis was born. He had a head full of curly hair and looked just like A'more. Only thing he had of mine were my eyes. I

never knew how good it felt to hold something that
you created. I loved A'more even more for giving
him to me.

"Aww look at him y'all. My god baby is adorable."
Chante and Rah had just walked in and my mom had
just left. I knew right then and there that I wanted to
be with A'more and my son. I just needed a way to
tell Tangela. I knew it would break her heart but my
heart belonged to A'more and probably always
would. Damn I was in a fucked up situation.

A'more

I couldn't believe that my son was finally here. The
look on Trent's face when he came was that of pure
admiration. He was a proud papa; too bad, we'd be
raising him in separate homes. Which by the way, I
had yet to find a place. I was staying with Chante and
Rah. Trent tried to get me a place but I wouldn't let
him. I had picked up a part-time job working at the
hospital as a CNA, but when I was seven months, I
went on maternity leave. I had a little money saved
from when I was with Trent and from my job, so I
was good until I went back. I just didn't find anything
I liked. Or maybe it was what I was used to. I
couldn't afford anymore.

I don't know how long I had been sleep but I woke up
to Trent holding Christian and it was cute.

"Hey. How you feel?" he asked me when he noticed that I was awake.

"Sore as hell," he laughed.

"Thanks ma, for giving me the best gift ever." I just smiled. That was cool until he went home to his girl.

Trent

Tangela was blowing me up. I had totally forgot about her, but I had more important things to deal with, like being here for A'more. I laid my son in the crib and went to A'more. I climbed in bed with her and looked her in the eyes.

"What happened to us ma?" she looked into my eyes with silence before speaking.

"You happened to us Trent. I wasn't enough for you. You had to go and sleep with your ex while we were together. So don't come with the pity party because you did this to us and then to add insult to injury you start dating before we even hashed out our issues." Damn I have to learn how to control my ego. I loved that girl so much it hurt. All I ever wanted was to do right by her but I fucked up time and time again. She didn't deserve that. It was best for me to walk away, because a nigga like me would probably only hurt her more.

*****

I was in a deep sleep when Tangela called again. I looked up and saw A'more asleep and the baby was in the nursery.

"Hello," I whispered so that I wouldn't wake A'more.

"Well damn we don't answer phones now Trent." Damn I wasn't in the mood for no bullshit.

"Man it ain't even like that. A'more had the baby and I was at the hospital with her. I apologize, but all I was thinking about was my son." She smacked her lips.

"You know what; all you do is talk about her. Why she do this and why she do that. I'm good, because I'm not playing second to ya ex. It's obvious you're still in love with her, so y'all go on and be a happy family and leave me out of it." She hung up. What the fuck was that about? I just shook my head because I didn't have time for that shit.

"Relationship problems?" I looked up and smiled at her.

"I thought you were asleep. Did I wake you?" I asked.

"Nah, I can't sleep with them checking my vitals all the damn time. Come lay with me Trent." I walked to her bed and laid down next to her. It was like old times when she would cuddle up against me and I'd play in her hair until she fell asleep. That was what I wanted back, but would it be that easy?

Chapter Ten

I Want You Back

Seven months later....

A'more

My little man was getting bigger and bigger every day. I thanked god for him because he was really all I had. Trent and I had been broken up for almost two years but they say you never forget your first love, and that was so true. I loved that man with everything in me but hey, if you love something enough, let it go, and if it's meant to be, then it will come back. I hoped that was true for me.

I had just finished getting Christian ready for his daddy to pick him up. That was our weekly routine. He would come get the baby three days during the week and Saturday. I was still with Chante and Rah but I had a few leads and planned to be out soon. Even though they say, it's no problem we still need our space and so do they.

"Ok pooh, let's go get your bag before Daddy comes." I grabbed him and went to the foyer to grab his stuff when I heard Trent's car.

Trent

At least my boy Rah and Chante were doing good with their little one. Armani was getting big. She was almost two years old and my baby boy was seven months. His mother was taking good care of him. A'more and I were over; I never thought I'd see the day where I couldn't stand to be around her ass. Even when we broke up last year, I was still feeling her. I wasn't fucking with Tangela anymore, so a nigga was lonely as hell. The only person I wanted though was wifey.

That time though, it didn't seem like it would happen. We had been co-parenting Christian and it had been working. I wasn't dating anyone else at the moment, because even though I wasn't with A'more, I wasn't over her. I doubt if I ever would be. They say you never forget your first love and she was definitely mine.

Today I was picking Christian up from her. That was the one thing in my life that was right. A'more had been staying with Chante and Rah. I offered to get her a place because she was still the mother of my child but she refused my help.

When I pulled up, I called and told A'more I was outside. Minutes later, she came out with my son in her arms and his overnight bag. She was looking good as hell. She had lost a little of the baby weight but not too much. Her hair was bone straight with a part down the middle. My dick jumped. Damn that girl still did things to me. I got out of the car so I could grab the baby from her.

"Hey ma." I spoke to her. She smiled.

"Hey." It was like conversation between us was awkward now. We never knew what to say to each other. We had become strangers.

"I'll have him back tomorrow afternoon." I said as I strapped my son in.

"That's cool. Just call me because I'll probably be out and about looking for a place. It's time to give Rah and Chante their space." Everything in me wanted to tell her to come home. I had to get out of there because the longer I stood there looking at her the more I wanted her to come home. But I had another issue on my hands. I had just found out that Tangela was pregnant. It was bad enough that I had to deal with Mya trying to pin her baby on me. But I knew that there was a possibility that I was the father of Tangela's baby. I still remember when the test came back stating that I wasn't the father of Mya's baby. That was the best news I had heard in a minute.

"Well we're out." I got in the car and pulled off. I had to do something to get my mind off of A'more.

A'more

Damn that man was fine. He did something to me every time. If only I could turn back the hands of time. I watched them pull out of the driveway before heading in the house to get my purse and keys. I had to find my own spot soon.

I jumped in my Maxima and headed to my destination. I was on my way to check out a place in Westland. It wasn't as lavish as the house I lived in with my parents or the one I lived in with Trent, but it was a place. Sometimes we had to learn to humble ourselves and I knew it was only the beginning for me.

The apartment was two bedrooms, one bath, and 1200 square feet. A far cry from my two acres I was used to. I decided to take it so that Christian and I could be out of Rah's house. He and Chante needed their space.

I was sitting in the leasing office waiting on my credit report to come back when Trent called.

"Hello?" I answered.

"What you doing?" he asked.

"Looking at this apartment. What's up?" I asked him.

"Why? I told you to find a house for you and my son. I don't want him in no little ass apartment A'more. He needs space to move around." He was working my damn nerves. We weren't even together and he was still trying to run shit.

"Look Trent, I'm looking at what I can afford. He'll be fine, plus he comes to your house a lot anyway." Even though my name was on the deed when we broke up, I didn't want to stay in that house anymore. It was a constant reminder of our failed relationship. I even traded my Maserati in for a 2012 Nissan Maxima. I was learning to live within my means.

"Don't fucking play with me A'more. You know I will take care of you and my son so cut the bullshit ma. This is the last time I want to have this conversation. Go home; I'll be there to pick you up so we can go find a house." Then he had the nerve to hang up on me. I stared at the phone for a minute in utter shock. That nigga was too damn cocky. But I loved it.

"I apologize for wasting your time, but I won't be needing this apartment." I walked out and made my way to my car. It was sure to be an eventful day. I hadn't spent a minute alone with him in a long time.

When I pulled up Trent was already there waiting. I got out of my car slowly and walked towards his. This was going to be awkward. When I got in, he was on the phone.

"Well I gotta go, I'll hit you up later," he ended his conversation and looked at me.

"We'll look around in Bloomfield and Canton at some houses. If we don't see anything, I'll contact a realtor in the morning, but it's time to get out of Rah's shit and I want you and my son living comfortably." If he really wanted us to live comfortably, he would tell me to come home. That's what I wanted to say but I didn't. I just sat and enjoyed the ride.

"You good ma?" he asked.

"Yeah I'm cool," I replied without even looking at him.

"Well after we look at a few houses we can stop and grab a bite to eat, cause a nigga ain't ate. You know I don't get home cooked meals no more since you gone." Was he trying to give me a hint?

"Damn, ya bitch don't cook for you?" I couldn't resist. I had to know if he was still fucking with that broad Tangela.

"I don't have a girl. It's just my son and me when he comes over. Shit, truth be told, no one compares to you ma." I heard him talking but where was this coming from all of a sudden.

Chapter Eleven

Was It Worth It?

A'more

So two months ago, I moved back in with Trent and things were going good. Well at least I thought so but I found out that that bitch Tangela was pregnant. Now I knew it happened while we weren't together but I found out from her. She called to tell Trent about her appointment. What a fucking way to start fresh huh. Well I was tired of bullshit from men. I really had some decisions to make. I could have handled it if he would have told me about the baby, but he didn't. I found myself in front of Marvin's house. Why his house, I didn't know but I needed a place where I could think without Trent.

I knocked on the door and he opened it up and smiled.

"Come on in ma." He stepped to the side and let me in. If I knew the consequences of me going there then I would have never come. But we all have to fall and bump our heads sometimes.

Marvin

Damn I couldn't believe my luck. That nigga had fucked up and there I was alone with my ex bitch. I had ran into her a while ago and apologized, you know threw it on extra thick. Just like a female, she went for it. I wasn't really into playing captain save a hoe but that bitch did me dirty for that nigga and payback was a bitch.

"So what's the deal with you and homeboy?" I asked her. She was upset and vulnerable so I knew it would be a piece of cake.

"I really don't want to talk about it Marvin. I just need a place to lay my head, where Trent won't find me. Please," she begged.

"Yeah that's cool." I needed her to calm her nerves so I pulled out a blunt that was laced with cocaine. Yeah, I was about to hit that for old time's sake. Fuck that nigga Trent. He took what was mine.

"Here, hit this and take the edge off." She shook her head no.

"Come on baby girl, just like old times. I'm just trying to help you calm your nerves." She took the blunt and hit it a few times before she choked on it.

"Slow down ma. Take it easy, that's that Kush," I told her. I knew it was the combination of the weed and the cocaine. Not even five minutes later, she was feeling it. She started telling me how she went against her daddy for that nigga and he cheated with his ex and some other bitch. I didn't give a fuck about that shit. I just wanted to fuck.

"It's cool baby girl. I got you." I slid over towards her. I took her face and made her look at me.

"You too damn fine to be dealing with this shit. You smart as hell and got a lot going for ya self ma. Fuck that nigga. He doesn't deserve you." Her eyes were drooping and she was hanging on every word I was saying to her. Next thing I knew I leaned in and kissed her lips and she didn't resist, so I let my hand travel up her shirt and played with her nipples. A soft moan escaped her lips and I took that as my cue to keep going. Before I knew it, her clothes were on the floor and she was begging me to continue. So I did. I snatched her thong off and pulled my dick out. This shit was about to be nice.

I pushed myself in her and almost lost it. Her shit was official and I hadn't even started. I slowly pumped in and out of her and I had to control myself because I was on the verge of cuming prematurely. Her pussy was tight as fuck. She was enjoying it as much as I was. At least the look on her face said so.

Damn. I couldn't control myself any longer, I nutted all up in her. Maybe she'd end up pregnant with my seed. Yeah that would fuck that nigga up for real. I pulled out of her and headed to the bathroom to wash up. I smiled at the thought of Trent's bitch in my living room. Just then, I got an idea.

When I walked back into the living room A'more was out of it. I laid down beside her and snapped a few pics. I got Trent's number from her phone and I sent the pics to him of his girl butt ass naked next to me. Yeah paybacks a bitch.

Trent

I was asleep with my son lying on my chest when I heard my phone going off. Considering it was three in the damn morning, it had better been A'more with a damn explanation.

I opened the text and immediately saw red. That nigga had the nerve to send me a pic of my bitch and him. I was about to murder her ass and him. I laid my son in his bed and went to the basement. I needed a blunt and a drink. I couldn't believe these muthafuckas had played me. All that time she crying boo hoo over me cheating and there she is fucking her ex.

I rolled a blunt and poured me a shot of Hennessy. I thought about everything A'more and I had been through to be together. Yeah I knew I cheated on her but damn, did she have to go fuck her ex. On top of that, I get pics of that shit. Yeah, I was good on shorty. I called Chante to watch Christian for me.

After she told me she'd be there shortly, I called A'more's phone because I needed some answers from her. No answer. All I could think about was her riding him like she did me. Thirty minutes later Rah and Chante was at the door.

"Thanks y'all. I'm sorry to call so late but I have to go and get A'more." They looked confused.

So I pulled out my phone and showed them the pics. Chante covered her mouth and looked away.

"Damn bruh, she doing it like that?" Rah was just as pissed as I was.

"Yeah man." I really didn't know what to say.

"So what you wanna do bruh?" I wanted to go to that niggas house and drag her ass home but if she didn't want to be there I wasn't going to force her. Fuck her.

Before I could answer, A'more walked in the door. I snapped. My hands went around her neck so damn fast. I could see her face losing color but I didn't let go." It took Rah to get me off her ass.

"It' ain't worth it dawg. A'more maybe you should leave and come back later."

"Why? This is my damn house and he's the one putting his hands on me, for what? I'm not the one that keeps fucking cheating! He is." I lunged at her lying ass again but Rah was there that time.

"Get the fuck out you trifling bitch!" She looked at me with hurt in her eyes but that didn't mean shit to me. It's one thing to cheat but to do it with her ex and then let that nigga take pictures. That shit was foul.

"Fine. Let me get my son and I'll leave." I stepped in front of her.

"I don't think so. Get the fuck out my house." The look on my face told her not to challenge me. She took one last look at me and walked out the door and my life. Damn, I couldn't believe my shorty did me dirty like that.

"You alright man?" Rah asked.

"I'm good bruh. Y'all can go. Thanks for coming." He shook his head.

"Anytime bruh. Come on Tay let's go." She hugged me and told me she was sorry. Why, I didn't know, unless she knew about this shit. After they left, I went to the basement to workout. I needed to do something or I was going to kill somebody.

A'more

I couldn't believe after everything I had put up with, that nigga put me out and disrespected me. He was the one that kept cheating with that bitch Mya and he went off on me. I had enough to deal with. I woke up in just my bra and panties at Marvin's house. He swears up and down we didn't do anything but something told me different. I knew I was never smoking with his ass again

I checked into a hotel. Tomorrow I would go and look for a place to stay. Hopefully he'd be calm by then and I can go get Christian's and me things, because if he thought he was keeping my son he thought wrong.

I woke up to the sound of the phone ringing. It was Chante.

"Hello?" I answered.

"Hey girl where are you, because Trent packed all your stuff up and asked me to bring it to you." What! That nigga done lost his mind.

"He did what?" I asked and she repeated herself.

"What the hell is going on Chante? I didn't even do shit and this nigga acting grimy."

"Uh he saw the pic of you and Marvin boo." What the fuck!

"What pic?" she told me and I was still confused. Then it hit me. That nigga took a pic of me when I was sleep. Fuck!

"Trent had a pic sent to his phone of you and Marvin. What the hell happened sis?" I didn't even know how to explain it. I was caught up in some real drama and had no clue how to fix it.

"Can I call you back sis?" I really didn't feel like talking anymore. I had to get shit right with Trent.

"Yeah. Call me back later." I hung up with Chante and laid back on the bed. Could shit get any worse?

Chapter Twelve

Four months later...

Trent

It had been four months since A'more and I broke up.
We were doing a good job at co-parenting Christian. I
had to admit though I missed the hell out of her ass. I
was on my way to pick up Christian. She was at
Rah's. She had found an apartment in Westland. I
didn't like it, but she wouldn't keep the house I had
bought her and when we broke up she decided to sell
it and I put all the money in her account, which she
doesn't touch. It's as if she wanted nothing from me,
even though she was taking care of my son. She still
has the job at the hospital but that shit wasn't no
money, but I couldn't force her to take my help.

When I pulled up to Rah's house, I called A'more to
let her know I was outside. She came out with my son
in her arms. She was looking good as hell. I got out
and grabbed the baby out of her arms.

"Hey ma." I kissed her cheek.

"Hey." Damn I missed her ass.

"What you got up for the day?" I asked making small
talk.

"Nothing."

"Oh ok well we'll be back later." With that, we left.

Chante had explained to me what really happened between A'more and Marvin but my thing was, she shouldn't have gone there. If she had an issue with me, she should have come to me. I was her man not that Marvin nigga. But it is what it is.

A little birdie told me that A'more was getting high, and I had ears everywhere being that I used to be a street nigga. To say I was pissed was an understatement. I was ready to fuck her ass up. I had someone following her so that I could find out for sure. I never in a million fucking years pictured A'more as a fucking crack head. But the signs didn't lie. She was always fidgety and she had lost a lot of weight, on top of niggas spotting her at the trap.

I was riding down Seven mile when I got the call I had been dreading. A'more had just copped from an old worker of mine. That shit hurt to the core to hear that she was out there like that. How long, I didn't know. I told them niggas not to sell to her ass anymore and I meant that shit.

*****

"I never want to see you again. You are a poor excuse for a woman and my son will not be raised by you. Stay away from me you selfish bitch!" I kicked A'more in the ribs, as she lay helpless on the floor. I

couldn't believe she did that shit, and she had my son.
I walked away and left her ass where she lay. I let it
be known that anybody that sold to her was signing a
death wish. How the fuck did shit get so fucked up?

Three months later

A'more

I couldn't believe what my life had become. I went
from being a rich kid from the suburbs to a damn
cocaine addict. I had lost the love of my life and my
son. My father wanted nothing to do with me and my
mother tried to help whenever my father wasn't
home.

I hadn't seen Trent or my son in almost a year. The
words he said to me the last time I saw him will
forever be etched in my brain.

*"I never want to see you again. You are a poor
excuse for a woman and you will not raise my son.
Stay away from me you selfish bitch!"*

You would have thought his words would make me
want to get clean but that was four months ago and I
was still using. All that did was make me sink into a
deeper depression. I needed help and I didn't know
who to turn too. As I lay on the floor of the drug
house, flashbacks of me giving birth to my son, my
graduation, Trent's proposal along with other things

ran through my mind. I needed a fix and didn't have it. I had run through all the money in my account and even sold my car for drugs and now I had nothing.

My body began to shake and I was cold even though it was damn near ninety degrees outside. I sat there going through withdrawals. I wanted it to stop. I wanted to hold my son and lay in Trent's arms. Lord help me. I passed out.

Trent

When I got the call from Eddie telling me that he had found A'more passed out on the floor, a horrible emotion took over me. It was embarrassing as hell but at the same time, I knew I needed to get to her and help her. As much as I wanted to leave her ass there, I couldn't. We had a bond that wouldn't allow me to turn my back on her. I still loved her and was going to do everything to help her.

I dropped my son off to his godmother Chante's house and made my way to where A'more was.

When I pulled up Eddie was waiting outside.

"What's up bruh?" He greeted me.

"What's good man? Where is she?" I asked getting straight to the point.

"She's inside. Look man I know you still love that girl. Help her through this shit man. This isn't the

A'more we all know. I don't like seeing her like this man."

"Thanks for calling me." I made my way into the house and when I saw A'more lying there, I almost cried. That was my heart right there and I vowed at that moment that I would do everything in my power to help her. I picked her up and took her to my truck. I was taking her to someone that could help her.

"I got you ma, believe that."

I took A'more to my mom's house in Chesterfield. My mom was a nurse and knew exactly what to do to help her detox. By the time I pulled up to my mom's house, A'more was in the back seat throwing up. I got out and helped her out of the car.

"Come on ma, let's get you better." I picked her up and carried her inside.

"Hey ma," I spoke to my mom who was expecting us.

"Hey sweetie. Take her to the guest room and I'll be right up." I did as she said and took her upstairs and put her in the bed. As I was undressing her, I noticed that she had a fever. That scared the shit out of me. First the vomiting now she had a fever. I ran downstairs to my mom.

"Ma she has a fever and she was throwing up in the car," I said concerned.

"That's normal with withdrawal. Which leads me to believe she's been going through this for a few days.

"Ok so what do we do now?" I asked.

"You leave and let me do what I do. I'll keep you updated but you need to be there for Christian." Hearing my son's name let me know I was doing the right thing by helping his mother. I prayed that we would prevail in the end. We had to.

Epilogue

One year later

Trent

All the shit we'd been through to get to that point. The cheating, the abuse, and the drug addiction made us stronger. Our baby boy was now two years old and we were expecting our second child. We were getting married and I couldn't have been happier. A'more was my heart and I couldn't have asked for a better wife. She completed me. She even accepted my son with Tangela. That was love right there. We had overcome the obstacles that tried to tear us apart.

I was on my way to pick A'more up from the salon. We had a date that night. I wanted to give her flowers while I had the chance. Show her how important she was because the next time I might not be so lucky. When I pulled up to the salon she was walking out with the brightest smile on her face. She was glowing; pregnancy definitely agreed with her.

Her smile instantly dropped. Before I knew what was happening gunshots rang out and she hit the ground. I jumped out the car and ran to her but it was too late. She was gone. I could feel it. Why did shit keep happening to keep us apart? I looked up and saw Marvin with the gun pointed to his head. I wanted to shoot him but I couldn't even move. I was afraid to walk away from A'more.

POW! He shot himself in the head. What the fuck!" I heard the sirens in the background but I still couldn't move.

"Sir we need you to let go of her so we can take her."

I ignored everything they were saying to me. A piece of me had died. How was I going to tell my son his mother was gone? And the baby she was carrying; did she make it? Why me, was all I kept thinking. I knew everything happened for a reason and we aren't to question God. I blamed myself because if I had been there for her she would've never felt the need to go elsewhere. But it was too late, my shorty was gone.

More by Demettrea Coming
April 21

Look for more books Leo Sullivan Productions LLC

Coming April 10th

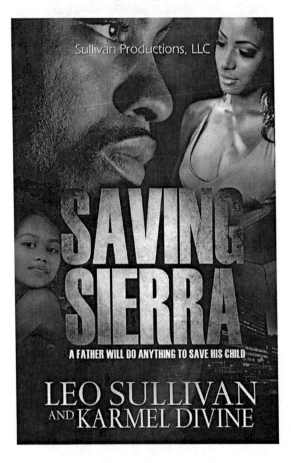

Coming April 30th

Check out books already out....

More to come…..

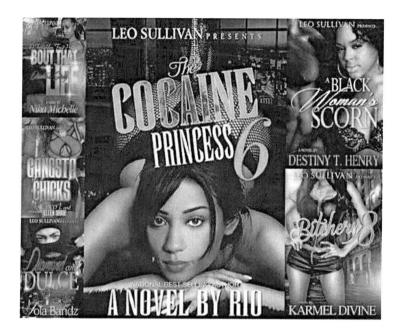

CPSIA information can be obtained at www.ICGtesting.com
Printed in the USA
LVOW07s1334040116

469043LV00017B/460/P